Suzy Ceulan Hughes – The Western Mail:

'This is a powerful and impressive prose debut from Davies, who uses her command of imagery as a published poet in the cause of stories that are sometimes shocking but show a mastery of the raw forces of sibling rivalry.'

Brandon Robshaw – The Indep

'Deborah Kay Davies has achiev.   ....ching rare: a collection of short stories wherein each story is complete in its own right (many were competition winners, or radio broadcasts) but which also work together as a novella-length sequence.'

Alyce von Rothkirch – Planet:

'Deborah Kay Davies' first collection of short stories, Grace, Tamar and Laszlo the Beautiful, is a daisy-chain of short stories: each story is complete in itself, but they are also meant to be read as a consecutive narrative. The image of the daisy here is not chosen at random: like the flower, the stories are deceptively simple, concerned as they are with the everyday. But on closer inspection they reveal themselves as creations of beauty. They are perfectly pitched, elegant, observant and realistic in the sense that they describe the world without blinkers but without ever using language that is any way coarse, ugly or unevocative.'

GRACE, TAMAR
& LASZLO THE BEAUTIFUL

PARTHIAN

Deborah Kay Davies' latest novel *Reasons She Goes to the Woods* (Oneworld) was long-listed for the 2014 Bailey's Women's Fiction prize and short-listed for the 2015 Encore award. In her review for *The Guardian*, Eimear McBride described the novel as 'exquisite...to be marvelled at'.

When Davies' debut novel *True Things About Me* (Canongate) was published in 2010 the BBC TV Culture Show named her as one of the 12 best new British novelists. When the novel came out in New York in 2011, (Faber) Lionel Shriver in *The Wall Street Journal* chose it as her personal Book of the Year.

Deborah's first work of fiction was a collection of short stories *Grace, Tamar and Laszlo the Beautiful (Parthian)* which won the Wales Book of the Year award for 2009. Her very first book was a collection of poems *Things You Think I Don't Know* (Parthian) which came out in 2006.

She started writing when she was a mature student at Cardiff University, where she earned a PhD in Creative and Critical Writing and taught Creative Writing.

GRACE, TAMAR & LASZLO THE BEAUTIFUL

DEBORAH KAY DAVIES

PARTHIAN

Parthian, Cardigan SA43 1ED
www.parthianbooks.com
Published with the financial support of the Books Council of Wales.
First published in 2008
© Deborah Kay Davies
Library of Wales edition published xxxx
Reprinted 2019
Foreword © Becky Munford 2018
ISBN: 978-1-912109-43-2
Cover design by Marc Jennings
Cover photo by Gillian Griffiths
Typeset by Elaine Sharples
Printed by 4edge Limited

CONTENTS

FOREWORD

Nothing prepares you for reading *Grace, Tamar and Laszlo the Beautiful* – the unflinching look at the savagery and strangeness of girlhood, the insistent violence inflicted on the female body, the deathly pulse of sisterly rivalry. First published in 2008, Deborah Kay Davies' collection of nineteen interconnected short stories won the Wales Book of the Year in 2009. Set in the Gwent valleys, in a landscape that it is at once recognisable and otherworldly, these stories tell the messy, sometimes terrifying, coming of age of two sisters, Grace and Tamar. Although the stories appear in chronological sequence, they are separated by the passage of time and shifts in narrative voice. The narration moves from first to third person, and from the brooding, furtive perspective of the mother to the by turns immediate and taciturn viewpoints of the two sisters. These narrative movements capture the sense of fragmentation and disconnection shaping individual identities and familial relationships across the collection. But it is also from the gaps and spaces in and between narrative perspectives that glimmers of understanding, of sisterly love and sympathy, shine through.

The emphasis on perspective, on seeing things aslant (or not seeing them at all), is thematic as well as formal. This is a book that peeks and piques. The stories offer an oblique look at family, friendship, marriage, sex, desire; together, they create a multifocal view of the jealousy and disappointment, as well as the pleasure and discovery, that inflects the experience of growing up 'girl'. Perhaps most unsettling about *Grace, Tamar and Laszlo the Beautiful* is its undaunted gaze at the violence enacted on and between the two sisters, whose discordant relationship troubles

1

any romanticised image of sisterhood. In 'The Point', Tamar pokes out the blue eyes of her sister's doll, Valerie, with the sharp end of a compass. The proleptic image of the blinded doll, whose eyes are turned full circle 'so the pink backs were at the front' and then re-drawn with a brown felt-pen, only barely forewarns of the story's startling conclusion. Having pushed Tamar out of a tree, Grace finds her face down amongst the brambles. She turns her over to reveal a 'sharp beech twig impaled in her blue, blue eye'. The unhurt eye is still moving.

Images of looking, of peeping and prying, run through the stories and are associated foremost with the mother, who feels that she has spent years of her life '[s]pying, glancing, checking through nets and blinds and half open doors' in order 'to understand *something* she's actually reluctant to know' about her youngest daughter, Tamar. Indeed, Tamar is unfathomable to both her mother and her sister, Grace. In her mother's eyes, she is strangely unformed, 'almost human, but not quite there yet'. Vital and unpredictable, she is in a state of becoming. The vulnerability of her body is powerfully conveyed through the insistent attention paid to her skin, the fragile frontier between inside and outside that is bruised, grazed and cut as the stories unfold. 'Cradling Breezeblocks', for example, depicts Tamar's mother looking on as a rough block slides down her daughter's shins, 'peeling off a layer of tender skin' each time she drops it; and, in 'Whinberries', she watches Tamar run her hands 'through a clump of asparagus ferns' until they bleed. In a particularly chilling poetic turn, the cardigan retrieved when Tamar goes missing is described as 'a discarded skin'.

In contrast to Tamar's exposed, sometimes knickerless, unruly body, Grace is clean and tidy. The orderliness of her body is communicated through her clothing, which plays an essential role in establishing her sense of self – and the social presentation of her girlish and womanly identities. While Tamar is associated with the harsh surfaces of the natural world – with stones, branches, mud and dust – Grace is immersed in the culture of femininity.

She is fascinated by the textures of her clothing, by the 'feel of her new chocolate brown dress [...] with its six layers of stiff, dark petticoat underneath' in 'The Point' (in which she also experiences a 'secret gladness' to see that her sister's dress is dirty with garden dust) and the 'handfuls of cold chiffon' in 'Negligee'. But, the protection offered by these costumes is only ever precarious; these social skins cannot remain unblemished. The dark orange pollen smears left on Grace's blouse in 'Grace and the Basset Hound' are scant preparation for the story's harrowing denouement.

If this is a book about the chaos of sisterhood it is also one about the disorderliness of motherhood. The collection starts in a maternity ward with the traumatic birth of Tamar. Narrated from the mother's distressed postpartum perspective, it opens with an image of a distracted male doctor throwing disinfectant into the 'raw wounds' of her 'ruined' body. This is the first of a number of shadowy and menacing male presences in the text; the smell of antiseptic lingers in the collection, reappearing with the image of Tamar's heavily wounded body in 'Stones'. The representation of the mother's body as at once ethereal ('[s]he has calming out-of-body times when she rises up and hovers near the fluorescent light strips') and emphatically physical ('the gaping hole between her legs feels as if it is spanned permanently with barbed wire') captures the tension between interiority and corporeality that pervades the stories. But here the archetypal figure of the heroic and sacrificial Welsh 'mam' is deflated: Grace reflects in 'The Point' that her mother 'looked like someone who had had the air extracted from inside'; in a later story, 'Peckish', she is disgusted by her mother's gluttony, the sound of her masticating and the idea of her 'mouth puckering up, pale and secret like a baby's anus'. As the interrupted telephone call that structures this story suggests, the mother is unable to communicate with her daughters; for all of her spying and watching, she is displaced, inert, unknowing.

The disquiet that seeps through the collection is disturbed by a dark, but tender, humour. Moments of joy, of pleasure and laughter, ripple through the stories: the frissons of first love in 'Kissing Nina'; the warm twinges of awakening sexuality in 'Laszlo the Beautiful'; the contented self-exploration that opens 'Grace, Ivanhoe and the River'. Although the sisters' intuitive knowledge of one another has deathly turns (in 'The Point' and 'Thong'), it is also playful ('Fun and Games') and powerfully compassionate (in 'Stones' and 'Cords', the closing story). *Grace, Tamar and Laszlo the Beautiful* is about a love that endures. The intimate connection between the sisters is conveyed with a poeticism that is as moving as it is savage. In the end, it is the fragile, but unbreakable, 'cord' running between Grace and Tamar, who are 'at odds with each other' and 'strangely at one', that holds the stories together in a beautiful, messy completeness.

Becky Munford

STIRRUPS

Nothing has prepared her for giving birth to Tamar – the forceps, the stirrups, the sound of her own heart slowing down, the doctor squatting on his stool between her spread legs, stitching, stitching, and talking to someone out of her view about the squash game he'd played the night before. The way he threw disinfectant into her raw wounds, as if he were sluicing down the toilet floor. How he'd said to his unseen listener, I don't wish to brag, but I destroyed John. In fact, I was bloody invincible on court. If she could have disengaged one leg she'd have kicked him hard in his masked face, smashed his safety glasses into his eyes. Now all her visitors say, how lovely, another little girl, a playmate for Grace.

She misses Grace as she lies in bed with the strange, swaddled baby beside her in its cot. She longs to hold her first-born's solid, warm body, sniff the damp curls at the back of her neck, kiss her pliant lips. It seems as if all the pain of wanting Grace is centred in her throat. She can't swallow; the muscles feel rigid. She tries to massage them into life. The two years since she gave birth to Grace now seem to have been lived in some glowing, marshmallowy dream-country where nothing hurt; there were no sharp noises, no grief. Over and over she plays through the same fantasy: two tiny, golden-haired children run across a smooth lawn. Their smocked dresses flare out around them; their perfect feet are bare. She tries to imagine her two pretty daughters together, but she feels nothing will be the same again. Tamar's face with its tightly shut eyes seems to hold some knowledge that she can never hope to understand. She gazes from her pillows until her new daughter's face begins to look like a wizened little plum. She has no desire to pick her up.

She watches the other women in the ward. They all seem, with their crumpled babies, banks of flowers, and cards that collapse and flutter around them, to be complete functioning units. There is a tiny Indian girl in the bed opposite. She has given birth to an enormous boy who has a shout that cannons through the ward. Everyone but the tiny girl gets edgy when he cries. She tries to watch without being noticed as the girl leans gracefully from her bed to pull him out of his cot. Then she breast-feeds him. His head with its spiky covering of black hair obscures the girl's small, full breast. She sits cross-legged and reads a magazine as he sucks, his hand clutching and kneading her nightgown.

Nothing goes right. Her breasts feel heavy, as if they are full of small pebbles; the baby is not good at suckling. Her stitches pull viciously and sting; the gaping hole between her legs feels as if it is spanned permanently with barbed wire. She doesn't think it will ever heal. She feels ruined. She winces and perspires with every move she's forced to make on the unyielding mattress. Her body behaves in a different way now. Her wedding ring is back in its box. It won't even fit on her little finger. Her ankles are swollen and aching. She can't believe how chunky they look. If she presses them with her fingers, soft, putty-like indentations appear and linger for hours like footprints in mud.

She has waking dreams where she sees her nine-year-old self, clad in shorts and T-shirt, running endlessly and effortlessly through a springtime wood. She feels the ferns slap her bare legs, smells the elderflower blossoms as they bump her shoulders. She sees her pale hair bounce and sway. Now all her short blonde curls have gone. Her hair has died. When she looks in the mirror she sees how ashy it looks. And flat, like a helmet above her straight eyebrows. None of these things happened the first time around, with Grace.

She tells her husband she can't have any more visitors. Even you, she wants to say, but doesn't have the courage. She watches him as he wordlessly holds the warm, squirming bundle. He's lost in this new love. He plays with Tamar's curled-up toes. After

6

he's gone she pulls the floral curtains around her bed and gingerly gets back in. She lies down and cries, her tears silent and relentless. She feels as if she is relinquishing herself; her chest heaves, her nose runs. She has calming, out-of-body times when she rises up and hovers near the fluorescent light strips. She looks down dispassionately. She sees her own ugly, saturated mouth. Some invisible force is pulling its corners down. She doesn't recognise her sobbing, lumpy outline beneath the covers. She'd like to drift off and swarm over somebody else's bed. She cries so much her eyes become sore at the outside edges. She longs to be at home in her own green and cream room. She wants to drink ice-cold milk and eat sharp, chilly apples. Nothing is cold in the maternity ward.

The dark girl opposite has food brought from home. Her mother and father arrive each evening with stacked metal containers full of steaming, spicy-smelling tit-bits. As they feed the girl they keep up a murmur of conversation. The husband sits alone, a little way off. He gazes into the cot at the big, sleeping baby. As she watches them she tries to eat the hospital food. Everything is the same colour and texture; it doesn't matter what it happens to be called.

When it's time to go home she tries to keep the nurse talking. She wants to hold her capable, antiseptic hands and plead with her to come and look after things. The nurse puts the dressed baby into her arms. There you are, dear, she says; you'll be fine. Then she briskly walks away. When her husband comes she goes to the toilet and stays there for as long as she dares, resting her head on the Formica panel behind the loo. She goes back to her bed and checks the cupboard again. They have already stripped her bed, wiped it clean of her tears and sweat. The Indian girl looks up from her magazine and waves goodbye.

Outside the air is too much, too many scents, too boisterous a breeze. She senses her body contracting. As she walks to the taxi in the spring sunshine, she feels that her heart is weakened now and will always be so. Even though she knows this is not physically true, she pictures its walls thinning by the minute, about to tear and leak out her watery life's-blood. She lifts her hands to her temples and presses; her head feels about to float away like a weightless globe of dandelion seeds. Her knees tremble. Around her ankles she can still feel tight, hobbling straps.

There are clumps of primroses in the hospital flowerbeds. She notices how the daffodils look enormous, their mouths stretched wide to tempt early bees. The birds are screaming in her ears. She stands and watches while her husband puts the carrycot on the back seat of the taxi and straps it in. Tell the man to just drive around, she says to him as she slides into the passenger seat – I don't mind where. They head into the countryside. She meets the taxi driver's eyes in the rear view mirror. He seems to understand her. She looks out of the window intently. All the people they pass seem so normal. She follows each one with her eyes, twisting around in her seat to get one last glimpse. The baby starts to cry, a high screeching. We'll have to go home now, her husband says. He's looking around at her anxiously. Of course, she answers. Home now.

THE POINT

I want to tell about the feel of my new clothes on a Sunday school anniversary morning. One year I had a chocolate brown dress, and I loved the colour. I loved everything about that dress with its six layers of stiff, dark petticoat underneath. Cool layers crackling like wrapping paper that made me feel like a present, and how the layers insinuated themselves sweetly between my thighs, and the way those petticoats lay in rough panels of chocolate lace all around me, a satisfaction of dark, lumpy lace over bouncing underthings, and the wide sash holding it all in, safe, around my six-year-old waist.

There was an American redcurrant bush in our front garden; its smell dried out the insides of your nose – those bitter leaves, hairy and ridged. And my father with the camera, taking photos of me in the hot garden. Stand with the flowers behind you, sweet, he'd said; stand still as you can. And I stood like a small, lacy statue for my father. I would have stood all day, in my holy dress, my hair uncurling, drooping, in spite of my mother who'd worked with curlers and sprays. My mother stood like a navy and white column and waited for us to be ready, a smile wavering across her pretty face. I would have been happy to stand forever, with the tender ends of the redcurrant bush resting on my shoulders and the purple flowers falling like miniature bunches of grapes bump-bumping my hair. My smooth hair I could feel relaxing its curls in the sunshine and silence. All for my father to say to me, good, good, and one more – this one will be beautiful.

I want to tell about my sister, Tamar, four years old, who, unnoticed, sat in the garden dust and smudged her peach anniversary dress. I felt a secret gladness to see that her dress

9

was dirty, and she could not have her picture taken. My sister's hair had a cow's lick fringe that never would stay flat; my mother tried and tried with brushes and clips and water; then with a curious shrug she would give up. And how someone yanked my sister up out of the dust so that she fell and cut her knee, the cut looking so bright and raw against the warm frills and fall of her dress. So out of place, the worm of blood that worked its way down her leg and soaked her new white sock, collecting in a dark stain. And my legs, no scabs, but one bruise on my shin. I remember how I got that bruise, the smell of hot, thunderous pavement I tripped on after a sudden shower of raindrops – heavy, and shocking as an undeserved smack.

Often I would lie awake at night, before I shared the bedroom, and run my hand over the wall from where I lay in bed. My arm described an arc, my thin arm with longish blonde hair and a click in the elbow. The wallpaper was warm and felty, patterned with sprigs of roses and buds. Each bud had a spiteful face that stared out from behind a leaf. I enjoyed wetting the bed in that twilit room full of bird-song and spiteful faces. I waited in the warm, spreading patch I'd made in the bedclothes for my mother to climb the stairs and loom through the door. Hanging on the back of the door there was a deep-red dressing gown with a tassel tie. In the dark, when the streetlights were out, the dressing gown turned black and writhed. Then I listened for the sounds of my parents downstairs, each clink of china and chime of cutlery like a soothing pat on my cheek, lying there in the dark.

My father would run up the stairs, each step so light, after I'd thought about him long and hard enough. And when he was with me in my room he made it different, better. Shut your eyes, he'd say, and open your hands, and then he'd place a biscuit or a piece of heavy gingerbread or sometimes a cube of salty cheese in my palms. And the times he pulled my toes until the joints clicked, although my mother told him mildly, no, you'll spoil her feet, you monster. Does it hurt? she always asked. I would offer my toes to my father, and my fingers for him to bite. She likes me doing it, he'd say, not looking her way. He'd smile at me, whispering, you do, don't you, darling? My father had a black and white checked jacket with leather patches on the elbows and leather trim around the cuffs. It had an amber smell of wood, tobacco and mints. If I breathed that smell, everything was going to be all right, always.

I want to tell about my mother, who was twenty-six for so long. She talked to herself, nodding and smiling as she washed up and looked out of the window through the trees towards the mountain. She licked her pencil tip before she wrote a shopping list. In the evening she took her apron off and combed out her fluffy, pale hair. Don't touch my hair, she'd say; it's a thing I can't stand. You didn't have to touch her hair to know how soft it was. It smelt of sandalwood and fresh ironing. In the evening she sat like someone who'd had the air extracted from inside. She said, I wish a little sprite would come and do the washing up for me. She'd say this in a dreamy voice. Look at my lovely feet, she'd say, and lift them up slightly, the arches extreme, her toes so perfect. You haven't inherited my feet, poor thing, she'd say; take off your socks. And yes, my feet were thin, different, not nearly as nice as my mother's small, plump feet.

I had a doll, as a present for no particular reason, from my beautiful, beehive-haired, buck-toothed auntie, who had glasses with wings at the sides, who wore diamonds and had long red nails. She had pointy, ankle-turning shoes that scraped their metal heel tips on the path and sprayed sparks as she walked. My doll I named Valerie had coarse, platinum hair and lips so small they looked as if she disapproved. But I knew this wasn't so. One day my sister poked out Valerie's unblinking blue eyes with the point of a compass, blinded Valerie for life. My mother said, here, good as new, and turned Valerie's eyes full circle so the pink backs were at the front, and drew new eyes for her with a brown felt-pen. Then her eyes were brown and crooked, and the way she looked at me with those brown eyes, I knew she was a different person. I stuffed her in the back of the cupboard,

11

beside the yellow tartan kilt, behind the piles of crusts and other things I didn't want to eat.

Then my mother said to my sister, come here, bad girl, and say sorry. And she did, squeezing her arms hard around my waist, butting me with her head until I fell over backwards. There, friends again, said my mother; you forgive her, don't you? Then she turned back to the washing up. My mother's blonde hair glowed like a halo. Her lips moved, eyebrows lifting, as she talked soundlessly to the mountain through the window. I can't explain how Valerie was the only doll I ever wanted. Each time I thought about her squashed up in the cupboard I wanted to do something, but I couldn't decide what.

One summer morning I woke up and knew that a special thing was going to happen. Something that would change everything forever. I could hardly wait for the day to begin. Later on in the morning I thought perhaps I had been wrong. Then, in the afternoon, when the heat was so heavy it had choked the birds into silence, my mother called us out to where she was resting under the apple-tree at the bottom of the garden. She lay in a deck chair with her feet up on a stool, flicking through magazines. She was wearing a strappy, pink top tied with a knot at the front. The air was cool and green under the tree; gold patches moved about on mother's pale skin. In the grass she had a clear drink, full of blobs of ice. I want to tell how her voice sounded as she told us to go out to play – drowsy and mild. Now girlies, don't come back for at least an hour, she said. Stay together. And remember, she said, holding me gently by the wrist, you're the oldest, so take good care. We stood by the side of the lounger, not wanting to go. For a moment I longed to sit on the grass and look at picture books and watch our mother resting and quiet; it was so odd. Shoo, she said, buzz, and waved us away, her wrist in a beautiful droop.

I ran across the field outside our house and tried to lose my sister, but she clung on. Down by the stream it was shady. There were clumps of shining watercress and some plants with big

12

hairy leaves that smelt of mint. I made my sister eat them. I told her she must eat twelve leaves. They could be poisonous, I said. You've got to trust me. I watched her chewing on the sappy leaves. Her lips puckered, and green spittle collected in the corners of her mouth. It was dim like a cave down there amongst the tall ferns.

I started to climb a big beech tree I knew well. I told my sister it was too hard for her to climb, but she still followed. I could hear her puffing and scrabbling as she tried to keep up with me. For someone so small she was a good climber; she never got scared. Soon we were nearly at the top and stopped to rest. I sat back against the trunk of the tree and looked at my sister as she nestled on a branch. She breathed quietly but deeply. She was pleased to be so high up, I knew. I could see down through the fine mesh of trembling, veiny leaves to the little brown stream and the undergrowth. I could feel the ridgy skin of the tree through my blouse. My sister looked perfectly at home. Her chin was clotted with green saliva, the flesh underneath her eyes shining with sweat.

I lunged forward and pushed her hard off the tree. I sat and gripped the trunk, listening to her body crash and thump down through the branches. She didn't scream. Then there was silence. I want to tell what it was like sitting in the tree trying to hear the sound of my sister settling in the bushes far below me. A dog barked, and I started to climb down. My limbs were aching and wouldn't work properly. I fell the last few feet and hurt my side. I heard my skirt rip. She wasn't near the bottom of the tree. I searched the undergrowth and saw a scrap of gingham. I forced myself through the blackberry bushes and ivy. My arms and legs were stinging from the bramble thorns. She was still. Lying face down. One of her shoes was missing, her sock was hanging halfway off; her bare heel had a pearly sheen. Her hair was like a little crown standing out. Lying there like that, she looked like a different person. I had to turn her. I did it with my foot. She made a sound as she rolled over onto her back – half a sigh, half my name, Grace. She had a sharp beech twig impaled in her blue, blue eye. I don't know how far it went inside. I don't think very far. Blood was pooling. There were some torn, lime-green leaves on the twig. Her unhurt eye was moving. I think she was looking for me.

CRADLING BREEZEBLOCKS

Tamar didn't talk much. Her mother brooded about how she was always alone. It wasn't at all how she'd imagined things: cute tea-parties, playing house, mud pies. Bringing a group of giggling, adorable little girls, her own two and others, trays of fairy cakes and cherryade. She the beautiful, fun- bestowing hub of it all. But Tamar didn't seem to need anyone. Her mother told herself it wasn't natural for a little girl to have no playmates.

She tried to talk things over with her husband. She had to follow him out into the garden, and talk to his bent-over back. Go on, he said, weeding the lines of new lettuces, I am listening. She hardly took in the dusky garden, the bird song, the tinkly music from a far off ice cream van. She pushed her fists into the pockets of her apron and told him she thought she had the answer. If Tamar could be encouraged to play nicely with others, things would settle down. There was a faint smell of spring onions coming up from the earth. You worry too much, her husband said over his shoulder on the way to the compost heap. I've never bothered with anyone, and I've turned out all right.

She promised herself she would do her brightest and best to orchestrate friendships for her daughter with the other little boys and girls in the street. This was how she had started to deal with things; she talked to herself as if she were reading from a particular kind of book. A knowledgeable book. A book that said things like *brightest and best* and *little playmates*. But somehow things always ended in tears, though not for Tamar.

So her mother began to form her own theories about Tamar, but wild horses would not have dragged them out of her. She thought about these wild horses. She'd never seen any, but she could imagine being dragged by one. And no, she wouldn't tell her theories. But that was ridiculous. She didn't have to say anything. Anyone with any intelligence could look at Tamar and make up their own mind. She felt as if her brain was like one of those toy cars on an electric circuit. Buzzing around the carpet, weaving around the table legs and back again and again. Stuck to the track. Unable to stop. Horses and cars? She almost thought she was going mad. And why would the wild horses care about her daughter? It didn't make any sense.

She felt a kind of exasperated compassion when dealing with Tamar, and knew that was the limit of her maternal response. I probably don't love her at all, she thought, and was appalled. *A limited maternal response,* that's how the book would put it. That didn't sound as bad. She asked her husband's back if he thought she was a good mother. He was cleaning his gardening boots with an old knife on a sheet of newspaper in the kitchen. He turned around and used the knife to point at her. I'm sure you're as good as can be expected, he said, and went back to digging between his boot treads. Stop going on and on about things, he said. That's your trouble. Dried clods of earth fell with a raspy thump onto the paper. You're like a dog with a bone.

The next morning she watched her daughter from the kitchen window as she played alone in the back garden. Leaning with her hips against the piled up draining board, cup cradled in her hands, she listened to the radio. She thought about being a dog with a bone. But dogs enjoy bones, she thought. They love them. That's why they stay close to the bone they have. Some out-of-it women were singing euphorically about flying up, up and away in their beautiful balloons. She stood there until the song finished and her coffee turned tepid and bitter. A crooked little line described itself on the bridge of her nose. She had expected to feel more as a mother. 'Up, up and away' she sang blankly, as she threw the dregs of her coffee in the sink.

Tamar's choice of play-objects was so unsuitable. The book Tamar's mother was reading in her mind described things that

16

way: *unsuitable play-objects are to be avoided at all costs,* she read, and so she tempted her stocky and frowning daughter with all kinds of pretty toys. It made no difference; still Tamar played with her own favourite things. For as long as her mother could remember, at least as long as Tamar had been strong enough, she would carry around a piece of wood or, if she could find one, a heavy stone. She was not a demonstrative child, but she treated these unwieldy things tenderly, hugging and stroking them. When eventually she grew tired, she'd squat down and sway for what seemed like hours on end, her arms full, as one would hold a small but heavy baby.

Her mother habitually stole glances at Tamar from behind the living-room nets. She felt strange, spying in this way on a tiny child, and knew it was ridiculous, but she couldn't stop. She felt as if she were examining a specimen; something almost human, but not quite there yet. She broached the no-friends subject with her husband again one evening. He was reading the paper. She makes her own fun, that's all, he said. Anyway, she has Grace. But Tamar and Grace were at odds with each other, she knew that. And Grace was just as difficult in her own way. It wasn't safe for them to be left alone together – she'd accepted that now. I blame you, she wailed at him. I thought you would, he said. About the time Tamar was five, she finally made a friend.

The girl lived in a house at the far end of their L-shaped row. There was no way of avoiding this house; it was the only way out of the street. Each time they went out Tamar had plenty of opportunity to look at the fascinating girl. Her mother would try to distract her attention as they walked past, but no matter what she did, or how firmly she gripped her daughter's small, sticky hand, Tamar always contrived to twist and pull until she was free. Then running on ahead, she homed in on the gap she had made in the privet hedge. Eagerly she grasped the mossy fence posts, swinging backward with suppressed excitement, and stared with shiny, bulging eyes at her friend inside the garden.

Her mother knew better than to pull Tamar away too soon, before she was ready. She doubted her daughter would ever really be ready to curtail her wordless gazing, but usually after some time she could be pulled away without too much force, coaxed with a promise of a treat. One day, with a deep breath and the air of someone about to dive reluctantly for something at the bottom of a dangerous pool, the mother had looked into the garden.

The girl on the grass was tall and well-developed, perhaps fifteen or sixteen, with the pale, round face of a moon-struck child, puffy and indeterminate. She smiled and dribbled at Tamar and her mother. She wore men's Wellington boots and their weight pulled her feet outwards as she sat straight- legged. The garden was on a slight gradient, and her dress had worked its way up to the top of her spread thighs; Tamar's mother could see their pale gleam and the blotches caused by poor circulation. As she stepped back, her hand on her throat, she could just see the girl's hand moving down inside her pants, whilst the other brushed the grass back and forth. With a convulsive jerk she pulled Tamar out of the hedge, and instead of walking to town, spun around on her heel. *Be mindful of the neighbours*, she told herself as she tried not to run home. She fought the desire to slap Tamar's dry-eyed, screaming face. She found herself almost hoping that she was dislocating Tamar's shoulder.

Tamar's mother now spent most of her time spying. She

appeared and reappeared at different windows, like a confused Swiss weather woman. She knew she should take a grip on things but was incapable of even the simplest task. *Get a grip,* and *simplest task*, summed up her struggle. She left Tamar to her own devices more and more. One particular morning, as her mother watched, Tamar struggled through a section of rotten trellis and went behind the shed. Then just as her mother felt she might have to go out into the garden and find her, she reappeared, dragging a breezeblock. As she worked she hummed a wordless, monotonous song. In her struggle to pull the rough block out from under a pile of garden rubbish, she had dropped it twice.

18

Each time, the block slid down her shins and peeled off a layer of tender skin. From where she stood in the bathroom, her mother could see the rapidly spreading red patch on Tamar's leg. It gleamed like a warning sign. She saw how little this injury affected her daughter. She wanted to look away but couldn't.

In the quiet, hot garden, Tamar, stooping from the weight of her block, walked to a rusted pram and tumbled it in. She pulled the pram behind her up the steps and manhandled it through the garden gate. Her mother whirled around and ran to the front bedroom window. Tamar was pushing the pram toward the house at the end of the row; then she stooped in through the gap in the hedge. Her mother watched from behind the curtains until she saw the big girl, who as usual was sitting on the grass, rise and walk slowly to the hedge. Tamar showed her the pram and its contents. With surprising ease the big girl climbed the hedge. Hunching down, she held on to the pram's handle like a child out with its mother. Tamar turned the pram, and the two disappeared behind the last house in the street. Her mother walked back into her own dim room and, without taking her shoes off, lay down on the pink bedspread and shielded her eyes with her free arm.

WHINBERRIES

From where she stands, duster in hand in the twilight of the landing, Tamar's mother watches her daughter drooping around in the garden. It seems as if she's spent years of her life doing this. Spying, glancing, checking through nets and blinds and half open doors. Trying to understand *something* she's actually reluctant to know about her daughter. Tamar is doing the sort of thing she always does when she's been sent out into the fresh air and she's bored

– scuffing her sandals in the gravel, snapping little shoots off her mother's flowers. Just now she's sitting on a wooden bench intent on sucking her hand. She has cut the fold between her thumb and finger. Tamar's mother watched her running her hands through a clump of asparagus ferns. She watched as she'd held tight to the damp fronds for a moment. She's not surprised now that Tamar has this cut. She sees the wound streaked with green sap.

She turns away to flick her duster at spiders. Then she pauses again to peer through the nets. She automatically dusts the window-sill and sees Tamar grimace as she sucks her hand. She remembers the childhood taste of warm blood, cut through by bitter fern-juice. She knows the juice will make the insides of Tamar's mouth tighten; its sour taste will cause the blood to feel creamy on her tongue. Tamar still goes on sucking though; probably it's something to do. Her mother rearranges the drapes and moves away from the window.

As she sucks, Tamar looks up behind the house to the mountain. Although the mountain is near, she has never walked there. Today's gently rounded summit is the colour of her mother's bunches of dried sage. Every day she looks at the mountain and notes its changes. It sits above the house – both unreal and part of home. Up till now she has never thought of going there, but today, suddenly, she realises there is nothing to stop her. She could just go; walk and walk and eventually stand on the very top. The possibility flashes briefly, and then Tamar looks down and studies her hand. She thinks really it's too far.

Later that evening, her mother, dry-eyed, will remember seeing Tamar hunched up in the garden. She'll hold her daughter's summer cardigan tight against her body and tell her husband how Tamar looked out there, sucking. How every now and then she'd shake her hand and then put her thumb back in her mouth, how just once she looked up and gazed at the mountain. She'd looked as if she had never seen it before. The mother thinks if only she'd gone out into the garden then, taken a little strip of plaster, or called Tamar in to bathe her hand, perhaps given her some ice-cream. She remembers how she'd paused to look through the bedroom and then the landing windows, and how irritated she'd felt to see Tamar so absorbed, messing about on her own in the garden, her socks loose around her bony ankles. Spoiling the flowers.

Tamar had known all along how her mother was watching from above. She'd shaken her hand as if the pain of the cut was unendurable because her mother watched her, but she wouldn't look at her. More than anything she wanted something to happen. Something exciting and different. She didn't even mind if it wasn't nice, just as long as it was something. Her mother always said little girls had no business wishing their lives away. Enough unpleasant things happened every day without wishing for more. She'd grow up soon enough and know these things for herself.

Tamar watched her mother as she pursed her lips and talked on and on. She listened to her mother but didn't believe a word she said, not for a moment. Even waiting in the garden it was possible something could happen. Knowing her mother watched through the window made things exciting. It was like being a

21

closely-guarded prisoner, and mother was the warder. Tamar knew that really her mother would love for her to go out and play with the other children in the street; she was always arranging little visits with children she thought were her daughter's friends. She never gave up trying to make Tamar play with her older sister, even though she must have known it was a waste of time.

Tamar turned her back on the windows and walked toward the back gate, scuffing the stones, raising little puffs of dust. The gate was tall and locked, smelling darkly of fresh creosote. As Tamar walked nearer, the smell intensified. The gate would be tough to climb, impossible with mother looking through the window.

Tamar's mother has made her another healthy lunch; a hard-boiled egg, some crackers, a stick of celery. She tells her if she eats her egg and celery she can have ice-cream.

She knows Tamar won't be able to. Her mother watches as Tamar cuts the celery into tiny crescents. Tamar hears the clink her mother's spoon makes in her ice-cream bowl. She eats very daintily. Ice-cream is all she is eating for lunch. It is variegated ice-cream; tenderest pink, creamiest yellow. Tamar has eaten her egg and managed, though she was careful, to put some bits of eggshell into her mouth. They grate between her teeth. No matter how she tries, she cannot eat the wet celery moons. No ice-cream for you then, says her mother, as she whisks off the table cloth.

Later, around about midnight, still holding the cardigan, Tamar's mother thinks about lunch-time. She could have offered her soft bread and butter and cheese. It would have been so simple to give Tamar that. Tamar would have loved to eat a bowl of raspberry ripple ice-cream. She finds it hard to think of how she ate hers slowly, exaggerating each movement of the spoon. Tamar had sat quietly without looking up. The silence in the kitchen was so complete she could hear the crunching of eggshells as her daughter chewed. She's baffled now, unable to keep still, suffused with a wincing, stark regret. Why hadn't she relented, pretended it was all a friendly game? She imagines herself back in the kitchen, but this time telling Tamar to shut her eyes tight while she places a bowl of pink and white ice-cream before her. She could have sprinkled it with hundreds and thousands, poured a gleam of scarlet sauce liberally into the bowl. Instead, after listening to the crunching sounds Tamar made for so long, she'd said calmly and deliberately, go upstairs and clean your teeth. Don't stop till I call you.

An hour after lunch, Tamar's mother reminds her it's time to call on Tom. This is one of the arranged things her mother does. The afternoon is drifting slowly up and away in a dusty haze of hot tarmac and wilting roses when Tamar gets outside. Her mother had insisted she carry a cardigan. There seems to be no possibility of anything happening in amongst the small, redbrick houses of Tamar's neighbourhood. The hard surfaces make the air so hot and heavy it singes the insides of her lungs. The glaring warmth of everything makes Tamar think of leaves and water. She hopes Tom will want to go fishing. Tamar's friend lives near the canal. Tom thinks fishing will be a good idea. He has a fishing net and says they should see if they can catch some sticklebacks. Tamar is to carry a jar for holding the fish. She waits on the porch as Tom gets ready. She can hear Tom's mother; she has some friends around. They're laughing; there is a smell of cigarette smoke. Tom's family has a television. Tamar can see the strange flashes and bars of light coming through the open door to the lounge. No one is watching, but the women in the kitchen are all humming along to a song a dancing man is singing on a show. When he shouts '...What's new pussycat?' the women all sing along. 'Woh ooo, woh ooo woh oo' they hoot.

They are holding imaginary microphones, though Tamar doesn't know it. Then they stop and laugh at themselves.

Beyond the singing women the back door is open, and Tamar can see clearly through the house to the little children playing on the swing and slide in the garden. There is even a paddling pool. Tom's mother shouts up the stairs. She tells him to get a move on or his little friend'll start taking root. She's not angry at all. Such a slow-coach, she says, walking bare-foot to the front door, smiling at Tamar. She rests against the door-frame. D'you want an ice-lolly, lovey, she says in a cool, casual voice and ruffles the little girl's hair.

Tamar has to be very still. She wants to reach up and hold the hand down onto her head; it feels like an absent-minded blessing. Instead she says no thank-you. She thinks about the silent kitchen and the eggshells. Her mother eating ice-cream. The way things are. Tamar sits down on the porch tiles. The floor is a rich brown, smooth and chilly against her skin. The tiles don't shine like her mother's porch. She would like to live in this house. Tom has three brothers and a baby sister; his gran is always around, giving him sweets. They have a television that everyone can sing along to. She supposes this is what makes the house so different.

From where she is sitting on a stool in the kitchen, Tom's mother can see Tamar in the porch. The following week, when it's all over and she sees her friends again, she tries to tell them how she'd felt as she watched the little girl play with a cut on her hand. She'd looked so self-contained, so intent on what she was doing. Tom's mother tries to tell the listening women about Tamar crouched out there in the shadowy porch, how she seemed far too eager for a smile, like a little puppy. As she sits smoking, one leg crossed over the other, she can't put into words how she'd wanted to do something, make some gesture, somehow include Tamar. She sips her coffee and tells the other women how Tamar's never included in anything much. They all sit drinking in the sunlight, and no one says a word.

On the canal bank it is cool. The nearly-still water smells of weeds. Tamar lies on the bank and dips her forehead in. The water is brown; she can't see the bottom. She imagines two thin, hairless, pale-green arms snaking their way up from the oozy mud. She thinks she would gladly hold on to them and fall in, her body hardly making a ripple on the surface, her bulky clothes slipping away as she slides down, down. Tom doesn't

24

think this sounds nice. Think of all the dangerous stuff down there, he says; lots of rusty cans, and old prams. Big eels too. They decide to walk on and find some part of the canal where the water is clear. Tamar trails her cardigan in the dust. Tom walks on ahead; he's eager to catch something in his net. Come ON, he says over his shoulder. I'm not hanging around for you. Tamar walks slowly. It's shivery but airless near the canal. The trees meet overhead. On the path in front of her she can see blobs of quivering sunlight. As she walks they surge up and over her, as if the sun is melting and dropping from the sky. The bank nearest the hedge is sprawling over the path, luxuriant with wild flowers. She stops to watch a huge black and amber butterfly open and close its wings as it rests on a drooping foxglove spear. It looks like a velvet brooch pinned there. No one seems to be awake for miles around.

Tamar walks on. She has no idea how long she has watched the butterfly. She doesn't care where Tom is. Each step has become a huge effort. She has a blister on her heel. As she walks she stoops occasionally to pick up a stone. She puts each one carefully into her shorts pocket. Soon her pockets bulge. She walks to the place where the canal slips under the earth for a stretch. Above there is a little rise and some open ground. The hedge is broken by a stile.

Tamar notices someone is resting against the stile. She walks towards the person and then stops, standing quite near. She wonders if she should say hello. The person resting there is a man. He seems old. The sort of old man who would still wear a cap on a hot day, and a tweed jacket buttoned up. Tamar thinks it's funny how old people never seem to get hot. The man turns and smiles at Tamar, gesturing for her to come nearer. It's as if he's been waiting for Tamar to arrive. Tamar thinks she recognises the old man; he seems so friendly. Do you know me? she asks. The old man smiles again. Tamar climbs up and sits on the top plank of the stile. She can smell tobacco and mints from the old man's coat. It seems familiar. She and the old man just stand, looking up through the fields to the mountain. Tamar realises it's the same mountain that hides behind her house. From here it is easy to see how anyone could climb up from the fields. She can almost make out a narrow path. The man starts to talk to her about the mountain. He tells her there is an enormous lake up there, just over the other side. Hardly anyone knows about it. No one ever goes there nowadays. He tells Tamar that there are the most delicious fruits on the mountain, called whinberries. He says they are dark purple and holds out his thumb. They're as big as my thumb-nail, he says. Tamar looks at the old man's nail. It seems huge, ridged and very tough. Tamar touches the man's nail and tries with her fingers to bend the nail over. I'm far too strong for you, says the man, and smiles.

Moving a little nearer he rests his arm on Tamar's bare leg. The tweedy jacket scratches her skin. The man's arm feels heavy, too heavy for Tamar to lift off. The man is gazing at the mountain. Would you like to climb the mountain and pick those berries? he asks, not turning to look at her. Tamar gazes hard at the mountain top. It looks like everything she's ever wished for. She imagines lying down among the short, springy bushes and tasting the berry juice. She pictures the smooth, deep lake, brimful of clouds, like a milky eye. She would like to paddle in it. The old man climbs slowly over the stile and stands in the field. Come on, he smiles, let's go now. He holds out his arms for Tamar to jump into. Tamar leaves her cardigan on top of the stile and leaps down, sure that she'll be caught. She slips her hot hand into the old man's cold palm. Then they walk together up the narrow track toward the waiting mountain.

STONES

Grace slips out through the back door after the police call around. The sight of her mother is too much. She stays long enough to see the officer put Tamar's cardigan down on the table. She'd looked at the mound of soft yellow knitting from where she stood half-hidden behind the lounge door. She tried to make sense of the cardigan. She tried to read the signs. She saw some sticky buds stuck to its waist-band. She watched her mother's blue eyes slip down to rest on it. Everyone, the two policemen, her mother and father, were all motionless in the small kitchen. And on the table, near the sugar-bowl, Tamar's cardigan, like a discarded skin.

Grace runs through the woods that rear up at the edge of the playing field. She runs along all its little dirt paths. She visits all the places she can think of. The beech canopy above her deepens to a secret green as the summer evening progresses. She runs through the pain of her stitch, through the undergrowth, welcoming its cuts and blows, until she falls down the steep side of a stream and comes back to herself in a luxuriant clump of dead-nettles. The palms of her hands sting; she has lacerated them on the drooping ferns that loll across her running paths. She sits in the silted margin of the stream and dabbles her raw hands in the water. Her gingham skirt sucks up mud. She thinks about her sister's cardigan and shakes her head like a pony troubled by flies.

Grace pushes open the front door. Her mother sits on the stairs covered in shadows. Her father is leaning against the wall. No one shouts at Grace for being out late. No one notices her injuries. No one asks if she is hungry. Grace pushes past her mother. She sees again the cardigan, now in her mother's arms. In her room the darkness is soothing. She climbs under the covers fully-clothed, and rests on her side. She looks across at her sister's empty bed. The room seems different now. Better perhaps. Her own. She's drifting through sheets of half-sleep, dreaming her little sister is never coming back. Grace thinks she is to be the only one again. Then the bedroom light snaps on. Grace can hear talking; there is a sense something has happened. The house is full of people. Grace does not move her position in the bed. Her father comes in carrying Tamar. He places her carefully on her bed and tucks her in. Your sister's back, he says, and goes out. Grace and Tamar stare at each other. What happened? Grace asks. She looks at her sister's golden head resting on the pillows. Her hair stands out like a fluffy ruff.

She's had a bath. What happened? she says again.

Tamar puts her thumb in her mouth. Girls your age don't do that, Grace says. I do, Tamar whispers around the sides of her thumb. She turns to lie on her back. I went walking with someone, she said. An old, old man. He was my friend from the canal. We went to pick mountain-fruits. Grace asks, did you know him? There is no answer. We walked a long way, very hot, Tamar says, and he made me hold his hand all the way to the mountain top. Grace imagines her sister holding hands with an old man she doesn't even know. She can see her trying to pull free. The man would need to be very strong to hold on to Tamar, who never wants to hold hands with anyone.

I liked him, Tamar says very quietly. Grace has to sit up to hear her. He gave me sweets. He said there was a lake. So? says Grace. There is a long silence. Grace can hear her sister's even breath. You are so stupid, Grace says suddenly, and falls back on her pillows. To go with someone you don't even know. Tamar says, but I had my stones. As if this makes the difference. Grace imagines Tamar perspiring at the side of the old man, her pockets weighed down by stones that had taken her fancy earlier on the canal bank. She is always finding nice stones. It drives their mother mad. When they are all out together she makes Tamar

28

empty her pockets periodically, ignoring her screams. Now Grace imagines Tamar with the man. She sees her pulling away. Not frightened, but wanting to run in the grass. She sees the two figures walking purposefully up the shrubby mountainside, the only movement in the silence. What difference does having stones make? Grace asks.

Tamar says, as if in answer, I needed a wee. I told him not to look. He said we were nearly there at the lake, but I couldn't wait. Grace knows the brow of the mountain, the little blind lake behind its shoulder. She has been there with her friends. She imagines Tamar squatting down to wee, her blue cotton shorts bunched around her bare ankles. The immense, scraggy mountain all around her. The skylarks singing up in the clouds. Incurious sheep chewing sideways. Grace sees Tamar's figure hunched down, trying to move her feet out of the way of her own jet of warm wee. Where was the man? she asks. Grace finds it hard to imagine the man there while her sister goes to the toilet. He said he would stand guard, Tamar says. I told him not to peek.

The bedroom curtains move in the midnight breeze. Behind the house Grace knows that the mountain waits. He touched my bottom, Tamar says, and smiles at Grace from her nest of pillows. Grace can see her sister's tiny oval buttocks, pale amongst the scratchy ferns. She imagines the old man leaning down to cup them in his big hands. It's not funny at all, Grace says. Tamar doesn't stop smiling though. She puts her thumb back in her mouth and concentrates on sucking for a while. What did you do next? Grace asks. Tamar uses her fingers across her bedspread and mimes running. Then what? Tamar mimes climbing a tree. Grace knows Tamar is a good climber. And she runs fast. She sees her streaking away, and pulling herself up out of reach. The old man would never have been able to catch her. Tamar says, he tried to get me, but I threw my stones down on him. He fell over.

Grace can see it. The old man caught in a hail of sharp stones. Tamar throwing her stones down hard on his upturned face. Tamar untouchable in the tree's crook. Her sandals splattered with wee, her hair standing out in sweaty points. Tamar tells her that, when he was on the floor, she climbed down. She was going to run home. But when she saw him lying there with his head all bleeding she picked up a heavy stone and hit him with it to make sure he didn't get up and catch her. She says, I hit him a lot. He was bleeding more. After a while he stopped making sounds. Grace feels far away, listening to the small voice. She looks at her sister sitting up in bed. She is acting out hitting the old man's head with the big stone. Grace's eyes are so wide she feels they will split at the corners. Her scalp is twitching. Then what did you do? she asks. Then I ran down the mountain, Tamar says, but I was lost, and I fell and cut myself.

Grace gets out of bed and moves across to her sister. She pulls back the bedclothes. Tamar's legs are heavily bruised. She has stitches in both knees. Her face is cut. Black suturing snakes away up into her blonde hair. Tamar holds Grace's hands. There was blood on his lips, she says. Lots of blood on my big stone too. Then she pulls Grace towards her. Why are your clothes still on? she asks. I was waiting to see if you were coming back, Grace says. Tamar sits up and helps Grace take off her blouse and skirt. When they get down to her vest and pants, Grace says, that's enough. Don't your stitches hurt? she asks. Tamar is sucking her thumb again, and just shakes her head. Grace puts her feet up on the bed, and they each unbuckle a sandal, Tamar using her one free hand. Come in my bed, Tamar says, and lifts the covers. She smells of talcum powder and antiseptic.

Grace gets in stiffly and lies with her eyes open. She listens as Tamar starts telling about her dream. She says that they have a little baby to look after, in their own big house. But we're children, Grace says; we can't have a baby to look after. But soon she's sucked in; it seems so nice, and she's tired. They lie in the narrow bed and tell each other what their baby looks like, what they have in their house, what they eat. Eventually they fall silent. Grace stares at the ceiling, while Tamar snuggles up and goes to sleep, sucking her thumb.

KISSING NINA

Grace first fell deeply in love when she was ten years and six months old.

Until then she had only been practising, going through the motions. Not that she knew many of the motions. She could only watch TV kisses on other people's televisions, and her own parents never would kiss, that she knew for definite. Grace had thought about the best ways to kiss for a long time, long before she was ten even. She had started by kissing her pillow, at night. Instinctively she made her mouth as delectable as it could be, as soft and eager as she knew how. She took time to close her eyes, concentrating on the fall of her eyelids. She knew how they gleamed damply as they lowered; she felt them cooling as the night air breathed on them. She was aware of the way her thick, spiky lashes would first touch and then mesh together.

There came a time when pillow-kissing was not enough. Grace thought about who would be willing to practise with her; she needed a person to kiss. She had to be sure that kissing a particular friend would, in itself, be pleasant. It wasn't easy to choose someone, but Grace knew that, of all her friends, Nina was the only one suitable.

Nina was very pretty. The same build as Grace, with heavy, auburn hair that always felt cool. The sort of hair that wouldn't stay in hair-clips or ribbons, but dead straight, poured down Nina's back. Of the two, Nina was the leader, and so it was arranged. All through the quiet evenings, in the autumn and winter before the spring that led to Grace falling in love, while they were supposed to be doing school projects, she and her friend Nina tried out all the different sorts of kissing they could think of.

Nina kissed with a sweetly martyred air, eyes wide-open and vacant. Grace loved to kiss Nina's chilly, unresponsive lips. She began to take care about where she stood when Nina kissed her. She liked to lean against the bedroom door, back and shoulders cushioned by the soft, dark-red towelling of her dressing-gown. Before Nina started to kiss her, Grace would hold the edges of her dressing-gown sleeves tightly in her fists. Not long after Nina began, her kisses as light as falling icing-sugar, Grace would murmur against her mouth, harder, Nina, do it harder. She'd feel a weakness spreading down through her chest, a pleasure shivering on the very edge of fear, which centred in a thick knot between her straining legs. Each time, just before she felt she must fall to the floor, Grace would push Nina away and jump onto the bed. Nina's hair, falling forward on her face, trembled as if it were alive. Avoiding Grace's eyes, she'd go back to her books.

Years afterwards, the memory of the waiting stillness of the house, the warm, musty air of the bedroom, the way the darkening sky pressed itself like a lost, lonely dog against the windows, and most of all, Nina's wide-open eyes, candid as a baby's, were still vivid to Grace, and seemed part of the spring she first fell in love.

It was the end of January when Grace found out about kissing with tongues. She'd heard about it before in school but wasn't sure if it was true. Finally she was convinced that people really did it. Now Grace felt shy about telling Nina. The early evening, while she waited for Nina to come to study, seemed to go on and on. She thought about this kissing with tongues. She imagined how she and Nina would do it, what it would taste like. She was unsure of Nina's reaction. She might get mad, tell Grace to grow up. She was anxious about her parents; she could never be entirely confident that one of them wouldn't come into her room without knocking, with a drink or something to eat. Grace's sister was another big problem. Even though she now had the tiny box room for her own, she was always finding reasons to slide into Grace's bedroom.

But everything was perfect this evening. Tamar was staying at their grandparents' house, where she could watch television. She'd been talking about a pop band she was mad about called the Bay City Rollers. She'd even got herself a Rollers tartan bobble hat and smuggled it into the house. She kept it under her mattress. Grace imagined her now, sat on the sofa at Gran's with her hat on, watching the band play. Grace's parents were intent on tidying-up in the lighted greenhouse. From the landing window she could see them hunched over pots and sacks. There was no danger of them coming in for hours.

Nina listened calmly as Grace explained about the new kissing. She asked Grace to swear she was telling the truth. They decided to do the new way of kissing that night. It was Grace's turn to kiss first. Nina's lips seemed different to her, hot and salty. She could feel Nina's lop-sided smile. Grace licked the smiling side of Nina's mouth and found the tip of her pointed tongue. To Grace, the taste of Nina, the feel of her sharp teeth, was delicious. As she pushed her tongue into Nina's mouth, she felt as if her whole life was concentrated there. She didn't want to stop. Nina's arms slid around Grace's shoulders, and they lay down on the bed.

In the warm quiet of the bedroom the radiator ticked. Snuggled on the pink candlewick bedspread, Nina and Grace felt suspended, waiting. They lay on their sides facing each other. Nina's breath, smelling as sweet as shortbread biscuits, lifted Grace's fine blonde fringe. They were quite still. Nina's brown eyes looked into Grace's blue, and Nina brought Grace's head close to hers, resting their smooth foreheads together. Can you read my mind? Nina said, and closed her eyes slowly, luxuriously. Linked at the mouth, they fell asleep. Grace and Nina did not talk to each other about the kissing and lying together. To them it was simple. They were very careful, even so, to keep it as their own special thing, something to be protected. But as spring slowly approached, and the evenings started to grow lighter and milder, they did not see so much of each other. There were so many other things to do outside. Soon the times they had spent together in the autumn and winter became part of the past – half-remembered, barely believed.

Grace loved to swim, and spent her Saturday mornings at the pool. Nina hated the water and never went anywhere near it. There was a particular boy at the pool, called Kit, whom Grace began to think irresistible. Secretly, she watched his elegant diving. She loved the way the water ran off his back, the way it made his pale hair darken, how he swam without splashing. She knew he watched her too. They didn't talk to each other, but gradually they began to swim together. Underwater they circled each other, slick legs twining. Once, Kit pulled her under towards him, where the water was six feet deep, and Grace silently slid down the length of his body, following its contours with her hands, her hair undulating above her. They looked at each other's eyelashes studded with seed pearls and watched the tiny bubbles escaping from between their lips as they smiled, the sound of the deep water like the pulse of some huge marine creature in their ears. They were evenly matched, alike in build and colouring.

One day, after they had silently swum together all morning, Grace found Kit waiting for her outside the swimming pool. He asked if he could walk her home. Grace smelt the chlorine drying in their hair; it made her dizzy. She held his hand, and they walked home together. At Grace's house no one was in. The air inside felt heavy and waiting, strange, like the rooms of a holiday home in winter. Grace felt like a visitor, no longer bound by the familiar rules that applied when her family was at home. She felt confident too, unable to put a foot wrong. The possibilities of the empty house seemed limitless.

Grace led him up to her bedroom. The winter bedspread had been replaced by a light cover, splashed with lime and yellow. The curtains sighed, lifted by a breeze from the open window. Spring sun slanted across Grace's legs, and she felt the familiar tightening and breathlessness in her chest. She sat on the bed and drew Kit down beside her. He smiled, the freckles on his nose stretching, and offered his lips. His kiss felt as sweet and smooth as a green grape. Grace drew back, recalling a hot, salty mouth on hers, and looked at the closed bedroom door. She remembered the warm radiator ticking on winter evenings, the cool hank of shining hair that slipped forward to bump her cheek, the shaggy embrace of her dark- red winter dressing-gown against the door. The light in her room was too bright. Grace shivered. Closing her eyes, she clenched her empty fists and firmly pushed the boy away.

FUN AND GAMES

The rainy Saturday afternoon has a spooled-out, used up feel. As she and Grace are squeezing into their best clothes, Tamar can't even be bothered to argue properly with their mother about going out. At lunchtime she drops her cutlery piece by piece onto the floor and announces she will not go to another ghoul's tea party, but her mother doesn't turn around from the sink. Tamar wants to stay with her father, mess about in his shed and play with his things, if he'll let her. She only half-heartedly tries to work Grace up.

After lunch there's a silent, intense struggle to get into her sister's room. Grace, reading out loud, rests her entire body weight against the door while Tamar pushes and grunts from outside. When, suddenly, Grace walks away, Tamar tumbles in and crashes against the bedside table. She hurts her knee, but that doesn't matter. She's there. Climbing onto her sister's bedroom windowsill, she drums with bare feet against the chest of drawers. Stop that, Grace says, without interest, still reading as she does her skirt up. Why don't you go for one of your long walks and never come back? Go and play with a brick, you'd like that. Tamar feels she should continue. Go and kick your own stuff, Grace says. Or I'll kick you. Hard. She picks up her brush and begins to listlessly sort out her hair, still reading.

Tamar slides down from the chest of drawers and throws herself on the bed. She lifts up her legs and allows her dress to crumple round her waist. She isn't wearing knickers. But Grace, she says in a sing-song whine, but Gracey-Grace, you know we're going to see that smelly man. You know the one I mean. Grace stops reading with a sigh. She looks at Tamar for the first time and says, for a small child you really are yukky. Tamar opens her legs and shiggles her pale, dry little genitals. Get off my bed, you make me feel sick, Grace says quietly. With force she throws the brush. It hits Tamar on the side of her mouth. Tamar gets up and leaves unhurriedly, trailing her hand across the bedside table so that all Grace's things fall on the floor. She sits at the top of the stairs for a moment and feels her lip with her tongue. Already the lip is swelling. She can taste her own blood.

The three of them walk through the rain. The girls have umbrellas. Under their brightly patterned roofs they look out at the downpour. Grace loves being under her umbrella. It's like being outdoors but in at the same time. She watches her shoes gradually soak up water, get darker as they walk along. The sounds of the streets are muffled by the thrumming of raindrops. The smell of rain makes her want to climb a wet tree and sit on a shining branch. Tamar flails her umbrella about, lagging behind. She stands under a broken down-pipe as they walk past the shops and enjoys the splattery water falling onto her shoulders. She slips off one of her shoes and watches it fill. Sky water comes gushing out from its mouth.

Her mother calls her name sharply, and she quickly empties the shoe and runs to catch up.

Neither of the girls wants to arrive, but their mother's in a rush to get out of the rain. Soon they are at the flat row of bungalows with their dull, secretive windows. Most of the gardens have flowers in borders, jokey bird feeders, wind chimes and stone animals. The one they want has a wreck of a front garden. An old bike lies in amongst the weeds. On its wonky handlebars sits a saturated crow that doesn't move as they hurry up the long path. He follows them with his eyes. Tamar wants to throw a stick she's picked up along the way, but her mother wrenches it out of her hand. Tamar notes where her mother drops it, for later.

They let themselves in, their mother fishing for the key that hangs on a dirty string from the inside of the letterbox. Go ahead, she says to the girls. Hurry up, why are you dawdling? She helps

Tamar take off her coat. Why must you always get so absolutely soaked? she asks resignedly. Look at your shoes. Get them off now. She gives her a shake. And what have you done to your mouth? Honestly, you look like nobody's child. Grace stares with narrowed eyes at Tamar. Your sister's quite dry, their mother goes on in an undertone, but oh no, not you. Grace and her mother look at Tamar dripping in the gloomy hallway. She looks as if she's been swimming in her clothes. She even smells like a stream. Tamar doesn't care. But she refuses to take her dress off, and starts screaming quietly when her mother tries to pull it upwards by the hem. I give in, her mother says to Grace. If she catches a cold, she only has herself to blame. She hurries into the front room, leaving the girls to sort themselves out. They can hear the TV, and a deep voice greeting their mother.

I never get colds, Tamar says, and makes a cross-eyed face, tiptoeing about with her hands in the shape of claws. I know you don't, says Grace. That's because you're not human. Yep, says Tamar. I'm not human at all. Then she stops and looks at Grace. What am I then? she asks. Grace considers for a while. It's quiet in the hall, and cold – hardly like a room in a house at all. There are wet leaves on the floor. Grace can see slug tracks shining on the doormat. Tamar slips her hand into her sister's. I haven't decided yet, but I have an idea, Grace finally says, and extricates her hand. Anyway, I'm not wasting my time telling you. Tamar seems content. Okay, she says.

Tamar has a certain look on her face. She seems a little excited, strange, Grace thinks. What's going on? she says, and quickly grabs at Tamar's wrist. She starts to give her a Chinese burn. What are you up to? I know you're planning something. What is it? Tamar is silent, but Grace can detect a glow like electricity coming from her. She is unmoved by the burn, and eventually Grace gives up. Tamar looks at her reddened wrist and rubs it calmly. I'm not telling you, she says. It's a waste of my time. She can do a good imitation of Grace's voice. Suit yourself, Grace says. Both girls start pulling wallpaper off the damp wall. They

38

hold up the pieces to each other. You win, Grace says, as Tamar waves a huge strip the shape of a cucumber.

The girls stay in the hall as long as they can. Eventually their mother comes and calls them. The room they enter is filled with a smell they don't like. A sort of muffled up, furry smell, sour and clinging, that makes them both twitch with distaste. There is a single bed along one wall, and this is where the smell is strongest. Instinctively the girls edge backwards and stand as far away as they can get. There is an old man in the bed, with an enormous belly that swells the bedclothes. Horseracing is on the TV, but the sound has been turned off. The miniature horses bob across the screen and make Tamar want to cry. She feels she'd like to have those tiny horses, and play with them in her bedroom. She imagines their sweet hooves tapping across her desk, the little horses leaping over obstacles. She wouldn't make it hard for them, just lay out things like pencils and sharpeners. She'd chop up blades of grass when they got hungry. She imagines washing them in a bowl of soapy water, how they would make faint, whinnying sounds because they were enjoying themselves so much. And they could sleep in her doll's house. She doesn't use it for anything else. Tamar is transfixed by the screen.

Her mother has to shake her to get her attention. It's only a television, she whispers. It's not magic. Then she says loudly, Tamar! And without meeting her eye, tells her to kiss the old man. Have you kissed him yet? Tamar asks Grace. Grace nods. She's looking a little pale. Tamar turns to the old man and says loudly, I don't want to kiss anyone today. But it's her turn, and Grace shoves her, so she leans over the bed, trying not to touch his body. She can hear his chest making noises that remind her of the faint calls of seagulls. He wants her to kiss him on his lips. They are a funny colour, surrounded by whiskers and beardy bits. Somehow she does it and gets away, but he has contrived to pinch the top of her thigh hard with his strong, horny hand. His spittle is on her mouth, and she shows him she is wiping it off with her sleeve. Tamar! her mother says again.

39

The girls go to sit on the floor behind an easy chair. They start playing with anything that's to hand; a clip, two coins, some elastic bands. They look at each other and make silent, exaggerated retching movements. With their eyes they say how they feel. Tamar's hair is drying into fluffy wisps. Grace's cheeks are shining pinkly. They can hear their mother and the old man. She is reading a lengthy story to him, and now and then he interrupts to ask a question. Behind the chair the girls sit cross-legged, fiddling with the bits and pieces they've collected.

They know the story well. It's their mother's favourite, about how a long time ago, a young blind girl becomes a missionary and travels somewhere many miles away, and then gets eaten by the natives. When they first heard the story, lying in bed together one night, their mother had cried at the part when the natives make a fire to cook the girl. They watched their mother with the blankets pulled up to their throats, and squeezed each other's hands under the covers; it just seemed too funny really to be someone's dinner. Just imagine, their mother had said, the poor, poor little thing. But she was happy doing God's will.

When they were alone they talked about how stupid that blind girl must have been. They agreed on the importance of at least taking guns and knives with them into the jungle. Grace said she thought God was a bit cruel, if that was really His will. God is very cruel, Tamar had replied. Also, she doubted the blind girl was actually happy being eaten. Grace devised a new game called Eyeballs after they'd heard the story for the first time. In the game they each took turns to try and prise open the tightly closed eyelids of the other using only their tongues. The one being licked had to lie perfectly still and not use her hands. If one of them succeeded, the prize was to lick the eyeball as many times as you wanted.

Then they'd swap places, and the other would try. Grace liked the saltiness and smooth curve of Tamar's eyeballs.

It was only a game for certain times, though, so now they zone out and concentrate on themselves behind the chair. Grace knows

Tamar is waiting for the right moment. Her face has blanked out, and her breathing is shallow. She squeezes Grace's fingers fiercely.

Their mother has gone out of the room to get a bowl of water and other things. The girls stand up behind the chair and gaze at the old man over its back. He gestures for them to come near. He rummages in the bedclothes and pulls out a bag of jelly babies. They watch impassively as he waves it feebly at them. His legs are moving in the bed, and he's smiling. We hate jelly babies, Grace calls to him. They make us ill. Anyway, we're not allowed to eat any sweets. The door swings open, and their mother reappears with a steaming bowl and towels. She wants the girls to help her. Grace has to hold the soap, and Tamar the towel. The old man is wearing a night shirt. He lifts the bedclothes to one side and exposes his legs, but the girls don't look. Instead they stare at each other across the bed.

Their mother washes his feet, and starts using clippers. The tough nail-rinds ping about, and the girls have to collect them into a little pile on the coverlet. Make sure you have all ten nails, their mother says. I don't want any working their way into the carpet. Then she buffs the cracked skin on his heels, lifting his leg onto her lap. The girls try not to breathe as the skin-dust rises through the air. They don't want to have bits of the old man inside them. Tamar looks down and glimpses, under the rucked-up night shirt, the old man's purply balls resting fatly on the undersheet. She doesn't really know what they are. He chuckles at her, but she doesn't smile at him. Their mother smooths cream onto his feet and massages them. He groans with pleasure.

Then it's time for tea, and their mother leaves the room again to go to the kitchen. Tamar and Grace can hear her filling the kettle and clinking plates. Okay, Tamar says behind the chair. I'm going to do it now. What? Graces asks. What are you going to do? Even if she'd wanted to, she knows she can't stop her sister. They both stand. The old man looks asleep. Tamar jumps up onto his bed and stands astride him. She starts to bounce the bed, bending her knees. The old man's eyes snap open, and he

41

tries to get his arms out from under the covers, but Tamar has them trapped by her feet. His round tummy is pressed against the tightly-held sheets.

She is bouncing near him, at about the level of his elbows, and he cranes to look at her. Grace moves to the side of the bed and watches as Tamar lifts her damp dress high above her waist. She is naked, and her body is without any colour. It looks like the body of an elf. The tiny cleft between her legs is like a neat, black, sealed-up cut. She squats for a moment, her knees spread, and laughs at him. She makes a face, pulling her eyes down with her fingers. He is silent, looking at her genitals, his lips pressed together.

Then she straightens up and bounces exuberantly over the old man, who has begun to make gurgling noises and thrash his head from side to side. His eyes are rolling back into his head. Grace can hear their mother approaching. Tamar, be quick, she whispers, and holds out her hand. Tamar leaps neatly off the bed, and with Grace disappears again behind the big chair, just as mother appears with a laden tray.

LASZLO THE BEAUTIFUL

It's the beginning of September. Indian summer weather. My first day at Secondary School. Terri and I both failed our Entrance examination in the spring. Trick questions, said Terri. Bugger the lot of them. Their loss. There is something very different about Terri. My parents don't like me to see too much of her. If they could see Terri now. Something has changed in the months we have been apart. I wonder if Terri notices anything new about me, but I doubt it.

Probably the last lot of new-cut grass lies in damp heaps on the school fields. Wood smoke hangs in the air. A stream of music drifts down, faint and sweet, from two skylarks up, up in the arching blue surface of the new-school sky. True-blue; the colour of my strange, stiff net ball blouse. Terri says it means good luck; two skylarks together stands for really excellent good luck. Two's very, very rare, she says complacently. She knows she's going to have good luck. My black lace-up shoes are dragging on the tarmac of the school drive, the surface already tacky from the sun. My shoes are so big I have to walk like I'm trying to tip-toe through a pantomime scene. This is the only way I can make them stay on. I keep getting stuck in the soft tar. I know I look ridiculous. Terri and I have new school uniforms on. I am wearing an enormous wool duffel coat. The toggles are plastic, though, not horn. The hem has been taken up three inches and makes the bottom of my coat bulky. As a result it doesn't fall properly. I know it will still fit me when I finish school. Terri wears a silky black three-quarter-length mac. It floats around her, held aloft by an invisible breeze. Her shoulder- length auburn hair is sprinkled through with red glints. It rises and falls like a bridesmaid's train, in time with the movements of her coat. Terri's shoes are patent leather. They have little perfectly-formed heels.

The school drive is long, and we're early. No one else seems to be around. I start to think, perhaps this is the wrong day. We'll look so stupid if this is the wrong day. Terri is sure it's a good idea to be early. Not too early, though, she says. That would be sadly eager. Just early enough to find a good place to wait. It's okay, she says. Our timing is just right.

Terri now knows about boys. She tells me it's because she has an older brother. She's spent the summer holidays hanging around her brother's friends. She's telling me as we walk stickily down the drive, about how one day she lay on a blanket in the back garden with these two really gorgeous boys who were going in the army soon. She lay in her bikini on the blanket, and they rubbed her with sun-oil. She let the really beautiful one feel her breasts through the bikini top. I imagine Terri with the big boy – nearly a man, she said – leaning over her. They are lying on the blanket her mother always takes to the beach. Terri lies quite still and reads her magazine while the boy rubs himself against her side. I imagine her smiling; she thinks boys are a wonderful joke, and of course she's in on it. I hardly think the other boy, the one she hasn't chosen, would want to rub himself against me. It was hilarious, she says. They had such hairy legs; you should have been there.

We reach the school play-yard. It's empty. Terri says we should sit on the grass ridge that borders the yard. It's a good position. The earth is so dry the grass scratches the backs of my legs. Terri's knees look brown between her high white socks and her black skirt. The bones are fragile and beautiful. My legs are pale by comparison, and thin. I have a concave scar on the side of my left knee. It's about the size of a Smarties lid. Under the surface I can see specks of gravel that weren't cleaned out properly. I got the scar learning to ride a bicycle that was too big for me. I realise Terri is already a teenager in her own estimation. It seems a big jump to me. She knows so much more. She's had her ears pierced since I saw her in July. She's wearing tiny ruby studs. Do you like them? She asks, and takes them in and out for me. I know your father's views on earrings, she giggles. Tell me about your summer, she says, her brown eyes squinting, looking around for boys. Anything to report?

I think about Terri's summer. Her mother out at work, so no adults around. All those beautiful boys, friends of her brother. Pop music I don't understand playing through the open windows. Her brother with a beer and a Playboy magazine, lying back on the lounger, sunning his acne. Everyone singing along to the song, everyone knowing it. Oil on her narrow back, polite hands, eager but not pushy, cupping her small breasts. And my summer, full of lemon- barley water, ferns, calamine lotion, stand-offs and stream-wading with my sister. The endless, dusty days. She and I strangely at one, keeping out of our mother's way.

The summer had been like a six week truce; I hadn't once tried to lose her. We were united in thinking up reasons not to be at home. Our mother newly caught, like a stick in an ice-lolly, by religion. I'd agreed to sleep in a makeshift tent outside on hot nights and drink warm squash tasting of plastic. In the mysterious back garden I even went along with the embroidering of our dream about the beautiful house and the baby Tamar and I shared. She was always on about it, and somehow, at the time, I didn't mind. So I have nothing to tell that Terri would want to know. Whatever, she says, looking sideways to scan the school driveway; I'm sure you enjoyed yourself.

Some kids from our junior school have arrived in the yard. Ignore them, Terri says; all that's no longer relevant; they're small fry now. What are we? I think. I feel like microscopic fry. Terri crosses her legs and lets her skirt slip up over her thighs. I make little dust mountains in the earth. My nails get dirty. The yard is filling up. Terri looks casual, but I know she's searching for talent. Don't look now, she says, but there's a beautiful boy over there. She pronounces it beeooduhfull. She makes it a long word. I can't do it. I've never tried, but I know I just couldn't pull off that word. Beeooduhfull. Long and longingful. She indicates with her chin where I should look.

He's standing in a circle of upturned faces. Spirals of laughter rise from the group. It seems he's highly amusing as well as handsome. He touches the girls casually on their backs, their arms; confident no one will shrug away his hand. Very slim, almost thin, and tall. Brown hair, cut severely short. Your father would like that haircut, whispers Terri, giggling against my cheek. I turn to look at her. The morning sun is to one side of us. I see for a split second what could be the promise of a moustache above her upper lip. The boy looks about fifteen and slightly foreign. I don't know why foreign, he just does. Glamorous and unattainable. Tanned from a season in some hot, hot place. I don't suppose he ever drinks lemon barley water. Beeooduhfull, I think, filled with an impossible, hopeless want. I'm sitting on the bank in my bulky black coat, my thin white legs poking out. My huge shoes drag my feet outwards. Terri's taken off her silky mac. She's smiling his way; she knows she's in on the joke about boys. I look at my little mounds of dust. Nothing seems funny to me. Secondary school is going to be more of the same, only worse. More secondary, somehow.

We settle in. Terri and I are mostly in the same groups.

For some, though, she's in lower sets than me. I'm with the comparatively bright ones. Different priorities, Terri explains shortly, shrugging, I'm into other, more important, stuff now, but carry on, you go for it. Still, I want to be Terri's friend. Perhaps I'm thinking something will rub off on me. People like to rub up against Terri, me included. I spend a lot of our break-times passing messages on to Terri: Neil says, will you go out with him? Brian wants you to know he thinks you're the most sexy girl he's ever seen, things like that. Terri takes her pick. Terri can get information she wants really easily, without even trying. When we are about four weeks into term, she's found out all she needs to know about the foreign boy. She tells me his name. Oh, I think, that just confirms his perfection, but I don't let Terri know

46

how I feel. I can never be sure how she will react. Perhaps she'll be annoyed and give me one those slit-eyed looks she saves for nerds and losers, maybe even deprive me of her company. After all, we both know it's only a matter of time before she gets him to herself. Or again, even worse, she might find the whole idea of him and me funny. But funny more in the pathetic sense. Sad, she'd say. Sad, sad, sad. I know it's sad, I don't need her to tell me so. She says his name is Laszlo. Weird name, she says. When she tells me his name, I feel faint. It's so right. Now, every chance I get I watch Laszlo. I can't help hoping he'll see me one of these days and understand.

I stop wearing the duffel coat, the weather is still so hot. It's October. There are dried-out foxgloves and fiery skies in the evenings. I'm on the way to school on my own. Terri is feeling ill. Time of the month. I'm seeing red, crimson tide, if you take my drift, she says, through a chink in the front door when I call for her. There are people in the house, music is playing. A boy is singing 'Fog on the Tyne' in a falsetto voice. Someone is calling her from upstairs. See you round, she says, and shuts the door with a bang.

Later, I'm walking down the school drive alone. Just as I come near to the gymnasium I hear a laugh, abruptly cut off. I follow the sound and walk around the corner of the building. There is a little secret enclosure. I see Laszlo. It looks at first as though he's listening to the girl who's leaning against the wall. His ear is up close to her open mouth. They don't see me. I'm invisible. It's quiet and warm between the buildings. There is a smell of creosote and trampled grass. I look down. Around my feet are hundreds of minute blue flowers. Speedwell, I think they're called. I hear a noise. It's the girl gasping. She is standing with her feet apart, pelvis thrust forward. In her hands she is clasping the folds of her skirt up to her waist, keeping them out of the way. My head feels light and about to float out of reach. My legs won't hold me. I know just how the girl must feel. Laszlo is still leaning towards her, detached yet involved. He nods. Yes, yes, he says softly, his accent strange. I see he has both his beautiful brown hands down inside the girl's panties.

The muscles in my belly contract strongly, taking my breath away. Then they relax painfully and slowly. I think I can't stand this feeling. It's so new and wonderful to me. A fist of intense joy rushes up through my throat into my mouth, choking me. I see a gold chain gleaming on his wrist. Everything is still. The only movement comes from his hands. They root up into the girl. Such strange, inevitable gestures. Her head lolls heavily to one side, her mouth twists. She opens her legs wider. Laszlo turns and sees me, the whites of his eyes glinting against his dark skin, the irises pale nutmeg. I can't move. He pulls one hand out slowly and carefully, as if not wanting to disturb anything, and raises it to his lips. Then he smiles and blows me a kiss from his shimmering fingers. Beautiful Laszlo, I say.

RADIO BABY

I'm pretty sure mother is going mad. There's only me to notice. Now the new baby is snuffling in the small bedroom on the top floor, well away from us. I stand and listen to the baby from the bottom of the stairs. Mother says to turn on the radio whenever the baby starts to wail. She says the baby doesn't mean anything when it makes that sound, just turn up the radio, for God's sake. If she suspects I'm moving to the foot of the stairs to listen, she calls me back and scolds me like I'm a six-year-old. I'm thinking, perhaps I am; perhaps that's what I want to be. When I tell her the baby needs her, that he's hungry and cold, she gives me the look she used to when I was little and had been caught out in a lie. There is a perfectly good explanation, she says calmly; the child is tuning in ahead of me.

I caught a glimpse of the baby yesterday, when mother arrived home. We weren't expecting her for another two days; she discharged herself ahead of time, phoning for a taxi, so father and Tamar were still at gran's. Me on my own for the first time. I had plans to clean the place up, maybe buy some flowers, at least get a meal ready, before she got out. I was in the bath, my hair thick with shampoo, when there was a knock on the front door. I stayed where I was; there are so many weird people calling these days, and I had no reason to expect anybody I knew. The knocking didn't stop, so I got out of the bath and ran to the half-open landing window and peered down. There was mother leaning against the porch wall. I could see her thin blonde hair flying around her head and the pink seam of her scalp, like a plastic baby- doll's skull. Under her arm she was holding a bundle; on the ground a big blue sack was sliding sideways. As I stood there with the chilled shampoo-froth snaking down my shoulders, I was so tempted to leave the door unanswered. I knew when that door was opened anything could happen. So I stood for a while watching, as mother shifted the bundle onto her hip and tipped forward to rest her forehead on the door.

In the kitchen I tried to hide the mountain of dirty dishes in the sink. I offered mother a cup of tea. First things first, she said, and manoeuvred the baby from her hip. It was a big, cumbersome boy with a rash across its upper lip. Mother unwound the bundle of blankets and dangled the baby over her shoulder like a little wad of damp laundry. I disliked the way its head lolled back and forth. His neck seemed too weak for the job. Mother didn't look natural with the baby, and all the time she held it, her face was contorted into what at first I took to be a smile. It came over her when she heard the baby crying; most people would have been fooled, but I'm not. After she had stood a while in the kitchen and looked at everything as if for the first time, she whirled around, saying she would put the baby in his place.

Mother has changed into her prettiest dress; marshmallow-pink with ruffles on the sleeves and around the hem. It's too wintry for this dress and her arms have erupted into goose bumps. I bring her a cardigan, but she says, no, it was so hot in there, she needs time to cool down. She hasn't washed since yesterday, and she needs to. If I get up close, I can smell souring milk and something else I can't identify. She refuses to answer my questions. I think she doesn't even hear them; she is listening for the baby, her body straining towards the hall, her mind's eye travelling up the long, unlit passageway until it stops short at the closed cream door. The pink dress is girlish, too tight across her breasts. The mound of her belly pulls the front up so that I can see her bare knees. She is seeping milk into the bodice. The drying milk leaves the material stiff. I can tell her breasts are sore; she cradles them tenderly in her crossed arms. Her face is flushed. I think she is developing a fever. All the time the radio plays. If she hears even the smallest scrap of commentary, she starts forward, instantly animated. Oh no, she says, no words, no conversation, no stupid chat for God's sake, and fiddles with the dials to find music. It would be good to find 'Moon River', she says quietly, but anything will do. When the room pulses with notes again, she subsides.

Neither mother nor the baby is eating. I prepare her favourite. A dish of baked eggs and cream. I take great care with the tiny triangles of toast. To make them look neat. But she looks at me with sly knowledge, as if she knows something about the food that I don't. The baby's cries have changed key, moved down an octave; he's tired of calling to her. When she fell into a brief, restless sleep earlier, I crept up and stood outside the bedroom. I tried the handle but it was no good, mother had locked the door. I haven't seen the key. From inside the room I could hear a faint, thin, grizzling sound.

Now mother is rushing round the house closing the curtains. Something's coming, she says, something very important. I ask her what, what, but she doesn't answer me. As she walks away, I see that smudges of blood are blooming in the seated pink fabric at the back of her dress – some fresh, some older and darker. Over her shoulder she says, we could go out, if it wasn't for the radio. I follow close behind. And the baby, I say; we mustn't leave the baby. She turns slowly to face me. Mmmm, yes, the radio-baby, she says, and nods, narrowing her eyes and tapping the side of her nose with an index finger.

Throughout the day the door has been knocked on several times. She indicates no, I'm not to answer, and blocks my way with her body. But mother, I say, it's probably the district nurse, come to check you are all right. She tells me not to be silly. A nurse? It's not as if I'm ill or anything, she says. She disconnected the phone when she found me trying to ring my father. Phoning will scrabble the soundwaves, she says.

It's late in the evening now, and mother has been perched for hours like some crazy bird on the arm of a chair in the lounge. Sit there, she coaxes me, pointing vaguely. The baby is silent. The radio is singing in the kitchen. Here in the lounge the record player is on. Messages are about to come through, she tells me. We must listen for instructions, make sure we're tuned in. I ask, will there be anything to tell us what to do about the baby? She slides down from the arm of the chair and reclines crookedly on the seat like a rag-doll, her legs apart. Her face gleams dully in the small light from the *on* switch. Keep still, she shouts, I'm about to take a message. Find a pen and some paper. I'm counting, she says in a playful, childish tone. If I get to ten and you're not back, I'll come and find you; then the fun'll begin.

Mother has counted to eight by the time I get back to the lounge. I sit opposite her and see she has been counting on her fingers. This way I don't make silly mistakes, she says, holding both hands up. We sit and listen to the radio. Mother starts to doodle on the paper, every now and then stopping to listen. I ask her what she's drawing. I'm portraying the child in the room upstairs, she says, and holds up the page. She has drawn a naked baby lying in some grass. From the neck down it appears normal, but where its head should be there is a radio. Notes float up from the radio's mouth. Then I see that instead of an umbilical cord the baby has an electric flex coming out of its navel. The flex floats up towards the top of the page and ends in an unconnected plug. I ask her, what does it mean? It's the radio-baby, she says patiently, as if I'm incredibly stupid. We sit on in the room. Mother struggles with the heavy record player and drags it onto her lap. The wires are pulled taut across the arm of the chair. She adjusts the controls. From out of her pocket she pulls a piece of cloth and starts to wipe the radio section with great care, patting and stroking it at intervals. Soon I'll know what to do, she says. I've only got to wait. The message will come through eventually.

I try to keep watch, but soon I feel myself falling, swooning into sleep. Through my dreams the radio plays, and far, far off, in amongst the notes, a baby cries, like a little interlude, and then is abruptly quiet. I wake up. The curtains are open and the radio is silent. There is an atmosphere of waiting that seems to tremble off the pale walls of the house. I hear mother treading heavily down the stairs. She pushes the lounge door open and walks towards me. I see a bright, wet smudge on her cheek. There, she says, giving me the bedroom door key and dusting her hands, I've turned off that radio for good.

GRACE, IVANHOE AND THE RIVER

Saturday afternoon. Grace is in her bedroom, getting ready. Under her pillow is a letter arranging a meeting today with a boy. Grace feels reluctant to look at the letter just now. Naked, she moves quietly from the chest of drawers by her narrow bed to the wardrobe. On the outside of the wardrobe door there is a mirror. Grace stands quite still, as if listening, with her head to one side. She takes time to look at her reflection. She cups her breasts in thin hands and weighs them speculatively. Slowly she lets her hands drop, not before making her small nipples harden. Her skin is uniformly white, bluey-white, and, as the bedroom is always cold in summer, corpse-cool to touch. Swivelling to the right, she sees the way her breasts look in profile. Fascinated, she discovers that a slight move sideways makes her right breast appear to swing away at an unlikely angle.

Grace's glance falls on a book on her bed. In a fold of the bedcover the title *Ivanhoe* in gold lettering shines from the dark-brown leather spine. If Grace's father could see, he would become angry at her treatment of the book. With a quick backward glance at her bedroom door she leaps, knees together, onto the book. She hears the spine crack, then lies on her side and presses it under her folded arms, until it begins to leave an imprint on her ribs. She closes her eyes deliberately, the better to smell the old dust shaken from the dry pages by her fall. She sneezes. With the book on her belly, she looks down to where she rests her palms on the small mound of pubic hair and senses her nerves, softly jumping under the pad of fat. The opened letter is under her pillow. Grace hears the small sound it makes beneath her head, but ignores it.

She slides off the bed and kneels up to peer at herself once more in the mirror, then, energetically, begins to dress. Her jeans are skin-tight – not real denim, too bright a blue, and lighter-weight, but this accentuates her lean legs and narrow hips; the fluid material drapes better. Her father won't like them, but he's not at home to see. She has to lie on the bed to do the side zip up, and then carefully move to a sitting position, like someone suffering from a spinal injury. Out of a bag she takes a new jumper, striped in maroon, cream and blue, and holds it up; it's a style she hasn't worn before. She puts it on, and pulls down the tight-fitting sleeves. She sees that her breasts are not big enough to affect the way the stripes lie. She makes a small nodding movement with her head, eyes steady on the mirror image.

Because she's ready early, she returns to the bed and lies down. Some pages have slipped from the broken binding of the book, and she spends minutes re-inserting them. The book is her favourite. She starts to read again about Rebecca, the dark, beautiful, imprisoned Jewess, but after two paragraphs she lets the book slide from her fingers and turns over onto her stomach. She pushes both hands under the pillow. Now she pulls out the letter and starts to read. A mild dread sifts through her. She tries again to picture the writer. He tells her they met last summer at a church camp, and that he loaned her his coat on a long group walk. He reminds her how they played table-tennis together one evening. She remembers the walk, but no coat, no particular boy who would lend it. She thinks about the table-tennis hut, the damp path, the fat snails crunching under her sandals. She recalls the rankness of the nettles, and the fragile, holey nets. But no one she played with there, no one she 'beat hollow'.

The letter says he has waited till now to write, not wanting to sound 'too eager', that he can't get her out of his mind.

There is someone knocking at the front door – probably the boy. She sits, motionless and listens to her mother welcome him in. She hears her mother call but does not answer. Only when she hears an unfamiliar cough does she get up and walk down the stairs. She looks at no one, decides not to take her coat, and walks out, with the boy behind her.

Grace starts to worry about her hair. Does it shine? Does it flow? She worries about her breath. She doesn't know her breath is sweet, or that her hair has touched the boy's cheek in the doorway like a glancing blow from a bird's wing, making him blink, making his mouth dry, making him blush, fixing his month-long dream of her. She can't imagine his sensation of fainting, how it combines with a clear, new, Technicolor vision of his surroundings.

Grace sees that, although the boy's clothes are stiffly new, he is carrying a battered little rucksack. It seems to sit comfortably on his back. She listens to the boy's voice; she has no idea what he says. His voice is deep; she doesn't recognise it. He asks her questions; she does not answer but goes on walking, head down, letting her hair glide outwards to shield her face. She watches her feet and sees the way her flat, soft, suede pull-ons crease rhythmically. She knows she must look at the boy, talk to him soon. Grace's mind has emptied, like a winter swimming pool. With a start, as if she has tripped and righted herself, she looks for the first time at the boy. He stops talking and stands still, a questioning look on his face. He blushes, looking down, discomfited and excited.

The boy is older than Grace thought; now, as she looks, she sees he is a man. With dawning recognition she studies him openly, and all the time he stands perfectly still, eyes lowered, lips slightly parted. She notes his crisp, black hair and pale skin, his strong beard, already shadowing the shaved chin. She lingers on a small, fresh, V-shaped cut on his jaw. The edges of the cut are slightly raised. His curling lashes flutter, each lash piercing the white, gleaming lid. She feels faintly nauseous, eager, not shocked to acknowledge a flare of cruelty in herself. The man opens his eyes, the colour of rust, and takes Grace's hand, as if something has been decided. They start to walk again. Grace longs to snatch her hand away, but does not dare. His palms are

56

warm and damp. She feels her skin both shrinking away and absorbing his sweat. She looks at the hand holding hers. Under the nails are new moon slivers the colour of graphite, and yet his hands are clean.

Again he starts to talk, and this time she tries to listen.

He talks about table tennis; has she played any since the summer? Of the place where he works, the long bus journey he took to get to her house. He asks about her family. Does she get on with them? These are not questions Grace thinks she will ever answer. His feet are small, almost the same size as hers. She realises he is only a little taller than she, but much bulkier. He tells her about the years he's spent working since he finished school, and how he is bettering himself, going to night-classes. He tells her, his voice lowering, about his desire to be a missionary, how it will make everything worthwhile. He starts to describe the sort of hot, open country he would like to do God's work in. Grace is incurious but polite, allowing her mind to drift.

They are now in an old lane. From the high banks, trees lean toward each other. The leaves overhead form a trembling, murmuring tunnel. It seems to Grace there is no air. The man's face looks drowned, his forehead glistening, his lips swollen and plummy. He pulls Grace towards him, then, pushing her backward, presses her against the trunk of a tree. Grace thinks her knees will buckle. Their eyes are almost level. He closes his tightly. He presses his lips to her mouth. Grace keeps her eyes wide and smells his breath through flared nostrils. She appears impassive. It's not until she makes a small, smothered sound that the man stops. He smiles uncertainly, gasping, slides his hands down to Grace's buttocks, and pulls her towards him. He nuzzles her hair, whispering her name.

Soon they start to walk again, and now the man is tongue-tied. Grace thinks perhaps she'll take him to the river, and then they can go home. She feels weak; the pulse in her throat is erratic. The man tells her how old he is, and his feelings about friendship. He smiles when he talks about his work-mates, and then goes on to talk about the age gap between Grace and himself. How it isn't really important; it's the way two people feel about each other that counts. Grace can hear him faintly and smiles and nods. It feels as if he is talking in some foreign language. The sky is overcast now and no one is on the riverbank. They wander off the path, down nearer the water's edge.

The ground is moist and the Japanese knotweed is giving off a rainy, astringent smell. Grace feels restless in places like this, green places, caves in undergrowth, amongst sprays of minty leaves; they awaken an empty feeling in her chest. Grace's jumper is low at the back, and she is getting cold, starting to feel hungry. The man opens his rucksack and pulls out a crumpled brown paper parcel. Inside are two apples. He offers one to Grace, and they start to eat. This could be nice, but the man's eyes are hot, and his fist, gripping the green, waxy apple, is shaking very slightly. Grace looks away; her apple has no flavour and is over-juicy. She slings it, with the skill of a boy, into the river and watches it circle and sink.

The heels of the man's small trainers are gouging lumps out of the earth. He is trying to reach across to Grace. She lets him embrace her, feeling calm, and doesn't protest when he kisses her, pushing down with his lips until she lies back on the damp bank. She feels the wet smack of the grass on her bare neck. She is aware that the zip of her jeans is slipping down and hopes the man doesn't notice. It seems to her that the clouds are moving at a frightening rate across the sky; the treetops whirl, urging them along. The man is breathing irregularly, exuding the smell of apple-juice. Grace licks his lower lip with the tiniest tip of her tongue and the man starts to moan, fumbling with his zip. Sitting up, Grace watches as he rummages inside his trousers. He pulls out his penis; the tip is trapped momentarily in a fold of clothing. Grace winces and helps him. She has never seen a penis before. The man's manner seems to call for some sort of response. Gingerly she holds it, aware of the life inside, the dark-blue, bulging veins. The man is transfixed; he frowns as if in pain.

Under the foreskin some small, frizzy hairs are trapped; Grace pulls them out, then twirls them between her thumb and middle finger. She feels a graininess. The man looks directly at her. He says, 'Darling...' and then, some moments later, with difficulty, '...It's all for you'. Grace sits, holding the shuddering penis for some moments, at a loss. Then he takes out a freshly laundered handkerchief and wipes his hands in it. He wipes her hands too. Grace stands and walks slowly to the water's edge.

Now there doesn't seem to be much to say. Grace and the man stand and brush themselves down. They do not look at each other. It's time to go home. They start to walk, and she becomes aware of the lightest mist of rain that seems to swirl around them. Grace senses the man is uncomfortable; he is trying to think of something to say. Each new topic he introduces she meets with silence. She can feel that her fingers are stuck together. As she walks, looking down, Grace is wording a letter in her head. In two days time it will unhurriedly glide down onto the mat in the narrow hall of the house he shares with his mother, causing him to fall into an exuberance of regret. And now the man has trouble keeping up. Grace is walking with energy, her head lifted, her eyes narrowed, the better to feel the rain.

THE WORM THING

I haven't always been this way, you know, the way I am now, about worms and earth, and to a lesser degree, teeth, pavements, things like that. I can remember a time when I positively, actually, really loved them (though perhaps not teeth, I felt fairly average about those). For instance, I'm thinking of the way I used to be with snails. If I tell you about the way I used to be with snails, then perhaps the thing about the worm, how it changed me forever, will make more sense. What I'm saying is, perhaps you'll understand. Perhaps you'll even sympathise, instead of thinking I'm some squeamish saddo who needs to get a life. So, I'll explain about the snails, and maybe also I'll touch on the toads and newts, stuff like that.

From way back, I had a strong thing going for snails. Preferably they had to be tiny; say, about half the size of my smallest fingernail. But if I'm honest, the bigger ones were also okay. What I'm saying isn't a contradiction; I raved over baby snails, and I also got a real buzz out of the granddads and grandmas; but only if they weighed heavy. I was particular about that. If I found a whacking great snail, there was no go if it was light; it had to be substantial and wet. The wetness thing may sound weird but it's perfectly under- standable. I liked my snails to be really healthy, you know, real goers. If they were drying out, getting light, I wasn't interested. They were no use to me at all.

Anyway, back to the minuscule snailettes. That's what I called them: snailettes. When you pulled those little jobs off a leaf, if you put your ear really close and stopped breathing for a couple of seconds or so, you could hear a soft pinging sound. That pinging tickled me to death. I never got tired of that little sound.

It was the noise the snail's oval, sucky foot thing made as it left the leaf. The big strong snails made a louder version of the same sound, equally as good, but in a different kind of way. Those little feet were so cute, so soft, grey and moist. You had to be patient and wait for them to relax. And I haven't mentioned the little horns. It's almost impossible to describe the way those four little shiny black horns would shoot out, the big pair usually a nano-second behind the other two. And the blobs on the horn ends, so incredibly cute.

Back to the feet now. You see, when you pulled it off a leaf the foot would go all hard and curl up around its edges. It didn't matter how gentle you were, this always happened. The thing is – and this is something people don't get – snails are so sensitive. Anyway, then you had to wait, holding the shell carefully between your thumb and forefinger. It was worth it though, the wait. If I tell you what I did with the snailettes, you may think I'm some kind of pervert, but I promise it was nothing like that. I'm going to tell you anyway, and you're entitled to your opinion. And the thing is, I wouldn't normally have told anyone, ever. I just want to.

So, after pulling a few chosen snails from their leaves and listening for the pings I've already explained about, and then after the waiting for them to relax, this was the thing I did. I would lie down and just carefully plonk the tiny snails on the bridge of my nose and close my eyes. The feeling of the moist feet wandering about was so neat. Sometimes one would travel across my eyelid, or they'd make their way up into my hairline. I remember this one snail slid across my lips, but that only happened the once. I didn't find keeping still hard, really. I suppose it had a calming effect. Sometimes the little fellas would venture up my nose. One got lost completely that way, but he was the only casualty. I never washed off the slime trails they left over my face and neck. After all, they were virtually invisible. It's true that in certain kinds of light they would gleam a bit, but never enough to be a problem.

I don't think I'll get into the stuff I did with the big, heavy snails; you probably wouldn't understand. I tried to explain to someone once before, and they freaked. People can be so closed off. When I was with my snails I had to lock my bedroom door and close the curtains. I needed my privacy.

That's what I did with my baby snails anyway. Nothing outrageous, just my version of getting back to nature in a meaningful way. It gives you some idea of how I felt about snails, though, the central place they had in my life. Now with worms it was different. Even more central really. It was a powerful feeling, this thing for worms. I loved to watch the worms – their coils, and the cute little soft ends, matching. I thought they were just plain beautiful. What I did was, I went out now and then – each time there was a rain shower, actually – and, as the pavements dried out, I did a tour of duty, picking up the stranded, dehydrating worms. Then I placed the poor things back on the damp earth. It didn't matter to me if some were as stiff and dry as little old burnt-out matchsticks; I could only do so much. I did try, when I was about eleven, to plump them back up by dunking them in a teacup of warm water, but it was useless, and I soon gave it up. The water in the teacup went a really interesting colour, though, so I added some sugar, and Grace and I gave it to our little brother to drink. We told him it was special, yummy stuff. Which it was really. Eventually it got so I couldn't stay indoors when a shower was drying up. I had to go out and check on those worms. Besides, I needed to get to them before the birds did.

There's nothing much to report about frogs and toads except that I loved them. Toads especially. I had this toad once. I found him squatting under a car outside our house. It was a wet evening, and I was getting restless about the worms, so I went out. Sure enough the rain had stopped. It was still and quiet, but I thought I heard a new noise close by, a sort of dry, lumbery noise. I traced the sound; it was coming from underneath a parked car. I peered under, and there he was. To be honest, I thought at first he was a particularly big dog turd, but then he moved slightly, splaying his warty claws. I could hardly breathe. I lay on the floor and held his claw. He didn't move. I wriggled further under the car and, resting my elbow in a pool of oil, looked at him. I thought the petrol fumes might be bad for him. We looked at each other for ages. Every so often he would slowly lower his eyelids over his mustard-yellow eyes. The thing that struck me was that he seemed so calm. I wanted him badly. All this time we were looking at each other, I had been holding his claw, so I began to pull. He didn't mind, so I pulled him right out from under the car.

It was like having the most wished-for but totally unexpected birthday present in the world, that first moment holding my toad. He was so heavy and dry, so lumpy and alive, with his cheeks going in and out and his eyes opening and closing. He gave me such a rush, I just stood in the dark street and rested him against my coat. One of his legs was leaning on me, his toes grasping a button.

I kept him under my bed in a special box for days, but the problem I soon encountered was to do with the incompatibility of my fave things. My toad, to put it bluntly, liked to eat my snails and worms. They couldn't all live in peace, man. Well, worms can live in peace with anything, but that beautiful toad, he only saw the others as breakfast. He had to go, even though I shed tears. But my overall point is this: I loved snails, worms, frogs and toads. I won't even try to explain about my two newts. I don't think I need to. Anyone who reads this will have understood by now how I felt about all these particular creatures.

Keeping this in mind, I think what happened to me seems even more awful, if you know what I mean. It had to do with my sister, Grace. She was into fishing in a serious way. Every time she went out fishing she came back all pale and peaceful. Not that she isn't pale and sort of pent-up peaceful most of the time. But she would be more silent than usual, more zoned-out, is what I mean. Her cheeks would be tear- stained because she got upset about catching the fish, but she couldn't help herself, because she wanted to touch and look at them close up. I suspect it was mainly the maggots that attracted her, but that's only my theory. We have that in common; what some would say is a compulsion to own wet, or at least damp, creatures. Probably why neither of us is that into our little brother. He's not ours anyway. He's our mother's own special property. *The precious one*, that's what we call him, but not often. Usually we don't refer to him at all. And I want to make it clear these are only my theories about the weirdo Grace. She's never told me stuff herself. But I think I'm right. We are sisters after all, and kind of understand each other.

This one day I was sitting in my gran's front room, reading one of those omnibus hardback editions of the *Reader's Digest* and half-listening to gran singing a medley of three different Sankey hymns. I was totally into those *Reader's Digests* at the time; especially the really grisly stories called 'Dramas from Real Life'. I'd just finished reading a story about this guy. He was a tree-cutter or something, and his big powerful chain- saw jumped off the tree he was felling and cut him almost in half. There was an artist's impression of him running through the pine woods, clutching his chest with blood splashing everywhere. His hair all caught in the branches. The whole point of these stories was that everyone survived, but I've got to say I was sceptical; it said he ran for five miles while he was virtually cut in half, holding his heart in his fist.

Anyway, I was sitting down finishing this incredible yarn. You must understand, things were always pretty peaceful at my gran's house. That's why I went there. I mean, my gran is the maddest person I know outside a mental hospital, but she's mad in the nicest possible way. Anyway, it makes her very soothing to be with. And she always feeds you up till you feel immobilised and stupid, but again, in the nicest way. So there I was, as full as a snake. I'd moved on to my other favourite article, a series *Reader's Digest* was running that genned you up about your vital organs.

Each month they would look at a different thing, and it was called 'I am John's heart', or 'I am John's liver' or 'I am John's pituitary gland' you know, medical info like that. I lived in hope of 'I am John's Reproductive Organs'. There was stuff I really needed to know, and there was always a diagram. This issue was 'I am John's Small Intestine'. I was really into the coloured illustration. In fact it was weird – I couldn't take my eyes off it. It reminded me of something, and I was trying to remember what, you know, like you do because it's bugging you, when my sister arrived.

As I've already said, we didn't have much in common, me and my sister, so I hardly looked up from John's intestine, and anyway, things seemed so quiet, there was no need. Gran was still in the kitchen singing about being in the garden of Gethsemane alone when the dew was still on the roses, in that nice, completely mad way of hers. I had just shut my eyes, feeling really mellow, when something tapped my foot. I opened my eyes, and there in front of me stood my sister, looking like she used to when she was concentrating on keeping within the lines in her colouring book. Sort of cross- eyed but not. I started to feel uncomfortable. I was into my own personal space at the time, and I felt as if she was seriously invading it. This was nothing new. I decided to ignore her, because of the mellow feeling, so I just shrugged and went back to my book. She tapped my foot again, and this time, when I looked up, she was smiling. This was seriously strange. Don't get me wrong, my sister was totally friendly with other people. It was just to her immediate family, and me in particular, that she was, at best, blank, and at worst, really hostile. Still, I wasn't expecting anything, what with the mellowness and everything.

I began, though, to feel something might be wrong with her. I mean, she was just standing there, smiling and smiling. The smile was just sliding into a grin when I noticed a speck of something dark between her lips. Then she was grinning widely and the black speck seemed to be moving, coming out of her mouth. It was hard for me to make it out, so I stood up and leaned close to

65

her. As I did she opened her mouth wide and out squirmed the biggest, blackest beast of a beautiful worm you have ever seen. She shut her mouth when the worm was half in and half out, and tossed her head back and forth so that the worm wriggled and wriggled. All the time my sister watched me, her switched-off eyes sparkling. Then like a flash, she opened her mouth wide and brought her jaws with their strong white teeth down three times on the worm and bit it to pieces. Then she started retching. All I can say is, I freaked. Totally. The next thing I remember I was picking up the *Reader's Digest* omnibus. I must have smashed it into her stupid face. She was kneeling on the floor, hands over her nose, squealing, while she spat little dollops of chopped-up worm all over gran's carpet.

SWALLOW

Grace can hear the clock tutting. Its pendulum slices through pure air. The organ pipes lean over, as if, like her, they are listening to the pews crack. She can smell the pews, each one exudes beeswax and pine. When Grace was a little girl she thought beeswax was the smell of God. Today, she feels that sitting in one of these serried pews is like sitting in a clean, dry forest on a windless afternoon. But she is not deceived by the benevolent smell of the pews. She was a baby once, scarcely one year old, who bit down on that resinous promise with two ridgey milk teeth. She still remembers her first encounter with wormwood and gall.

Today, it seems as if the pews are moving. Grace finds it hard to sit still. The wood groans as if it were a sheet being wrung out. The wood feels alive, bucking and rearing, intent on throwing Grace into the gap between the pews. But Grace is an expert at holding on to her dignity. She sits, unruffled. Her Bible is open at The Song of Solomon. The minister is reading: *like a lily among thorns is my darling among maidens*. Grace's father leans across and presses his pinstriped shoulder against her. He taps her page. She is in the wrong place. She looks at her Bible; it seems as if the love-thoughts are blossoming out from the page. Grace thinks no one understands them.

Words from the pulpit drift down and settle on the heads of the mute people, but they don't wipe them off. Grace's sister and small brother sit like effigies of children on the other side of her father. They are not really there, she knows. The congregation recognises the drifting words and are not disturbed by them. Once in a while someone will shift bulkily. Grace is watching the words as they slide down the backs of jackets and coats, and she notices something new; they stain the material as they dribble. Most of the words, when spoken in this place, turn ugly to Grace, and they make her shudder. She looks up, just to check there are no birds silently whirling around. The stains look just like bird-shit to her. But no, only a butterfly is up there, vivid blobs of crimson weighing its wings down. Even though Grace sits among the listening congregation, the falling words can't touch her. She knows she has a force field as flimsy as a rainbow, as pliant as aurora, in cool shades of blue and dove- grey around her. It wraps her up and keeps her free from smears and stains.

Grace thinks it's easy to fool these people. Especially her own parents. Not her sister, of course; she and her sister never fool each other. It would be like trying to fool yourself, only harder. But with the others you just move when they move, stare like they stare, sigh when they sigh, nod when they nod. It's all so easy. No one has ever doubted her. No one will ever know. Grace feels safe amongst these silent people, breathing in unison. All the time her shimmering skin makes her impervious. It gives her a feeling of energy, sitting here, hiding in the crowd. Even though she has to be vigilant, she feels secure. She thinks no one will expect to find her amongst her enemies.

It's dangerous, but Grace is playing a game. There is a rule that forbids games, so she does it quietly. She plays her little game without a sound, but she is never furtive. One thing these people know is furtive; they recognise it well. Innocently Grace is playing with her ring. It slips off easily. She thinks her feathery aura keeps her body temperature low. She must be careful. The ring has very sharp points. The game she likes to play is with the tiny stone. Even though she chose this ring, she doesn't feel comfortable with the way it looks now. If she studies it, Grace begins to doubt that she would ever have picked out such a ring. There are other things they say she has chosen, but she doesn't believe them. The strangeness comes from this ring's spiky nature; Grace wonders how something so circular, so smooth and butter-yellow could also be so sharp. Of course, that is its secret – a tiny, angry diamond standing proud of the soft gold, set atop a bunch of out-thrust platinum fingers.

This diamond and platinum crown is the important part of Grace's game. Without it she couldn't play. The pews have settled down, things are fairly quiet. Before she starts, Grace has to check, make sure certain things are as they should be: the words, the stains, the backs and shifting shoulders, the bending organ pipes. Today the pipes are truly spectacular. They almost distract Grace from her game. It is the colour that strikes her. Some days the pipes glow turquoise, like the phosphorescent walls of an underground cave, and the vents spit bubbles of saline water. Grace thinks sometimes she can just hear the faint cries of seagulls. Today the pipes are like tubes of terracotta streaked with cheesy amber. They have the texture of black pudding. From where she sits, Grace can hear them sizzling. She can smell the fatty meat. She tears her eyes away.

It's hard for Grace to maintain her equilibrium, but she's had so many years of practice. She thinks she'll need this expertise. She looks at the ring. She knows what it means. She knows there is no going back on her word. She has a longing for opals, pearls, moonstones. Perhaps even carnelians. Anything, as long as it is smooth. The diamond is winking at her, but she can out-stare most things. The trick is to bury the stone in something warm. Grace holds the ring in the palm of her left hand with the stone pointing inwards. Now she starts to press with her left hand. She is strong, and it doesn't take her long to puncture the soft skin of her palm. She doesn't stop pressing until the diamond is drowned in a pool of blood.

Grace's game is in two stages, and the first is complete. Grace sees the second stage as her reward. It takes ingenuity and a mild form of daring to complete. Casually she lifts her hand to her mouth, taking care not to lose any telltale fluid, and then swiftly she scoops the ring and blood together into her mouth. The gold, the stone, the smooth salt all lie in the cup she makes of her tongue. Grace wants the mixture to homogenise; she wants the ring to dissolve, but it hasn't yet. Concentrating on the idea of dissolving, Grace has a new thought. She can make the ring disappear. It's so easy. She lingers on the possibilities. She is sure that it would drift down and lodge in some red fold behind her heart. Grace imagines each heartbeat pushing it further into a plushy ledge. She thinks about how the flesh would grow around it, extinguishing that insistent wink forever. She relaxes the muscles of her throat and feels it slipping down, snagging as it falls. At the last possible minute, she coughs it up into her hand.

THONG

John arrived on his new motorbike. His head was so big – this I'd never noticed before – that he'd forced it into the crash helmet. I was interested to see how his cheeks were pushed forward and reddened by the pressure. It made him look like an angry baby. I wondered if this was something I'd always known, *deep down* – I mean, that his head was unnaturally large – and I'd just blocked it out? I decided I'd have to think about it later. Anyway, he said he'd sold the Fiat. This would be more economical. I listened to him as he said, if we were serious about ever getting married, we'd have to start tightening our belts. He says things like that – *tightening our belts* – but I'm working on it. Mostly I use ridicule to cure him of stuff. Just to make him understand that he often sounds like some old codger from the cast of *Dad's Army*. I find it very effective. I asked him if he'd rehearsed his bracing speech. 'Course not, he said, irritated. Economise? I asked. This from the guy whose idea of taking me out for a meal is sharing a bag of chips and a carton of curry sauce in the car park behind the chip shop on a Friday night. What are we going to cut down on, babe? I asked. He blushed a bit. He really is quite sweet sometimes. He opened and closed his mouth a few times. A bag of crisps in a bus shelter it will be, I said. You won't hear me complaining. Exactly, he pointed out – it's not a sacrifice, because of the way we feel about each other. I s'pose so, I said. He put his arms around me. I could see the marks on his cheeks from the helmet. Bless, I thought. Or not.

The parents were out – each in separate places – and the precious one was with Mum no doubt. Grace was up in her eyrie reading, or whatever she does to amuse herself, so we had a snog on the sofa. Just as things were hotting up – it takes John quite a long time to get going – in strolled Grace. Oh, sorry, she said, in that dead way of hers; I'm looking for something. I told her to push off. Don't be rude to your sister, John said, smoothing his shirt down. It's all right, I said; she doesn't understand English. Grace drifted over to John and wavered in front of him. I could see him starting to blush. I think it's under you, John, she said, and thrust her hand behind him. Her hair flopped into his eyes as she leaned over. It actually looked as if she was caressing his bum. No, she said, no, I'm mistaken, and wandered out again. John seemed paralysed for a moment. Then he got up and said he should be going. Please yourself, I said.

Usually I lingered on the doorstep. John liked me to wave until he'd driven off, but somehow that night I didn't want to see him ramming his head into his helmet. I didn't think I could keep a straight face, for one thing. For another, I had other stuff to do. I ran up to Grace's room. She'd locked her door, so I banged on it. There was no answer. What are you playing at? I whispered into the hinge. She opened the door, peering through the tiniest of gaps. I could see one eye and her long hair. God, calm down, why don't you, she said. Keep your wig on. I asked her again what she was doing. Reading now, she said. You'll have to be more precise in the questioning than that, dear. And while you're at it, wipe the foam off your mouth. You know what I mean, I said. The icky fumbling with John's arse. P'raps all that moony, pre- nuptial, semi-spiritual, virginy stuff you're into makes you so desperate you have to feel John up? Pass, she said, smiling, and shut the door quietly. I went to my room and put some music on very loud. I danced until I was exhausted and sharp, tiny stars exploded inside my closed eyes, then fell onto my bed and drifted away, thinking about stuff.

Grace started sunbathing in the back garden. At first I ignored her, but one day I was watching her from my bedroom window as she drifted across the lawn, trailing her bag and a towel, and I suddenly realised she looked stunning. Her skin was a delicate, pale brown; her long hair, lightened by the sun, flowed down her back. She had somehow acquired a cute and tiny bikini, which was actually a bit gorgeous. I wondered how she'd got that in under the noses of the parents.

I nearly choked. There she was, stretched out below me on the one ancient lounger we possessed, and she looked HOT. Of course, once I'd noticed this, and having a glass of orange juice in my hand at the time, I had to throw my OJ over her. It soaked her hair and book. Then I had to lock her out for a bit, because she was angry. The next door neighbour came round and said, this time she was going to tell my parents about all the nasty things I did to my sister. It seems Grace had climbed over into their garden and turned on the waterworks. You're both old enough to know better, but it's you I blame, she said, and pointed her finger at me. Your sister is so shy and quiet, the poor little thing. I shut the door in her face. I had no option.

We didn't speak for a few days. We had to sit in the lounge while I had a lecture from father. Grace shared the sofa with him, looking hurt and vulnerable. Not pale, though, as usual, because of her tan. Which was beginning to seriously get on my nerves. I'd always been the outdoorsy one, the wild, brown girl, and Spacey Gracy the white, wan, brainy one. I kicked her foot, but she wouldn't look at me. You girls only have each other, he said. It's a blessed thing, being sisters. Quite rightly, he didn't mention the precious one. Who didn't count at all. He made us promise again that we'd try and be nice. Our mother had long ago given up on the whole thing, concentrating all her surprisingly fierce love on you-know-who, but you had to feel a bit sorry for dad. He still felt there was hope. I'd tried to explain so many times. *Just because someone happens to be related to you, it doesn't mean you automatically love them.* Even Grace had talked to him, but he just couldn't accept it. We ended up promising to try and spend some time together, *bonding*, as he put it. The thing is, we are much too bonded. Way too much. But that doesn't mean we love each other.

John came around for a meal with us. He didn't look well.

Wassup love? I said at the table. You look a bit peaky. Is your helmet cutting off the blood supply to your enormous brain? Even mum looked up from her plate. Yes, John, she said, do you feel all right? He blushed. I love it when he blushes. It makes me go all strange inside. I want to be nice to him for a while. He told us he was having trouble with his sinuses. It seems that, when he's riding his bike, the dreaded helmet funnels the wind up his nose, and it's inflamed them. Very painful, apparently. Trust John to have sinus trouble. So unattractive, when you think about it. But Grace seemed oddly interested. She told the table at large that salt water was very good for this kind of problem. She sort of stared at John all the time she was saying it. John blushed even more. This time I just wanted to give him a slap. He seemed to be mesmerised by what Grace was saying. Have you tried salt water, John? she asked him. You should, but have you? Mmm? John dropped his fork and had to search for it under the table.

I stared hard at her until she looked at me. She was acting like some demented woman from a black and white film. What? she asked. Got a problem? I'm not sure yet, I said. Well, when you've decided, she said without emphasis, for God's sake don't tell me. I felt as if I was about to choke on my roaster. Thing is, she said, as if she was explaining something obvious to a very slow person, thing is, you see, I won't be interested. She took a sip of water. Not one tiny bit. My sight began to blur. It was a familiar Grace-feeling. I wanted to pick up the gravy boat and pour it over her sun-tinted hair. Then Dad pointed his knife at her and said, stop taking the Lord's name in vain, and stop being unkind to Tamar. She's younger than you, and not as quick. So I decided to jump in while the going was good and cry. Even Mum took notice. She looked up from stroking the precious one. How could you? she said to Grace, who sat there looking blank. But I knew, I could tell, she was absolutely burning. She looked down at her plate. The only movement was the trembling of her hair. From where I

74

sat hiccuping, surrounded by the sympathetic olds, I caught deadly mean flashes from her eyes.

Somehow, it was decided we would all go to the beach. Grace and some random bloke called Ben, John and I. Her fiancé was working weekends, she said. At breakfast one morning she'd asked me if I'd like to go. No, I said, and reminded her how much she hated the beach, how our father's idea of teaching us to swim when we were little was to grab each of us by a wrist and ankle, whirl us around until we were almost fainting and then let us go, into the waves. Children are like small animals, he said. Instinct will kick in. I reminded Grace that she'd seriously nearly drowned. Once, a lifeguard ticked Dad off for his dangerous behaviour. It was funny now, I said. Oh, really hilarious, Grace agreed, but back to our conversation. Say yes, pleeeeease. Stop begging, I said, it's too enjoyable. And wouldn't the sea-breeze mess up the pages of your book? Also, what had happened to her beloved? I'd forgotten what he looked like. And Ben? Who the hell was he? She said she didn't like her fiancé fraternising with her weird family too much, and Ben didn't count. She stayed calmly smiling all through the conversation, and told me she'd been really thinking over what Dad said, about us being friends, hence this outing. I studied her through narrowed eyes. Really? I said. Of course, she answered. So I said yes.

It was too late to acquire a tan. I tried to persuade John I needed a new swimming cossy, but he said we should both make do with the ones we had. I insisted he take me up to his bedroom to show me his. It was made of some shiny synthetic fabric. Is that what they call turquoise? I asked him, as I lay on his bed. Dunno, he said. But what do you think? The trunks were deeply naff somehow. It was difficult to pinpoint the actual reason for the naffness. Maybe it was the fake, toning fabric belt and tarnished buckle. I don't know. He stood there doing body-builder poses. He was pale but toned, absolutely in proportion. Come here, you stud, I whispered. He lay beside me, and I slipped my hand down inside his trunks. It felt wonderful in there. I wanted to kiss him.

Now you, he said, sitting up. Whatever, I said, and slithered into mine. Not too bad, he commented kindly. That's not exactly what a girl is looking for, I told him. I felt a bit stupid standing there in my ancient costume. He demanded I turn around. He said it was sweet, how you could see my bottom through the perished material. Actually I didn't mind. I knew I had a fab body. Speedo, is it? John asked. There's a subtle difference between economising and being mean, I said. You don't need a snazzy swim suit, he said. You look amazing, and pulled me back on the bed. Which was quite forward, for him.

We had to postpone the beach trip a few times. I almost forgot about it. Then suddenly, one Saturday, summer kicked in, and we were all ready to go. John was driving his dad's car. Early in the morning Grace and I bumped into each other in the kitchen. It wasn't a room either of us ventured into often. She seemed happy. I almost thought I detected her making a little humming sound. I asked if she was all right. Perfectly, thanks, she said, and went on making some elaborate picnic. Oh God, I thought, lunch hadn't occurred to me. I rummaged through the fridge and found some cheese. I felt it wasn't too late to make an effort, so I grated it before I shoved it into some pitta bread. Then I had a brain wave, and peeled it all apart to spread some pickle in there too. And some sliced tomato Grace didn't want.

I stood and watched Grace neatly doing stuff. Since when have you been Dame Delia H Smith? I said. Who? She said. She was chopping things. I asked her where she got her dinky little polystyrene containers. Can't remember, she said, and went on busily filling them with chopped things. And how long are you planning to be away? I asked. You've got enough there for a month at the beach. Be prepared, she said, looking at me a bit spookily; that's always been my motto. Really? I said. You surprise me; I always thought it was *be annoying*. Bonding, remember? she said, and put all her lovely picnic things in a new and trendy beach bag. What are you up to? I asked her. Just going to the beach, she said over her shoulder, and walked out.

We all sat in the car waiting for Grace to appear. Ben was quiet in the back. I asked him how long he'd known Grace. He said he didn't know her at all. So why have you agreed to come? I asked. It seemed to me a stupid thing to do; surely he knew she was engaged? Well, he said, sounding awkward, I wasn't going to turn down a chance to go out with Grace, was I? I mean, you'd be mad to, wouldn't you? Point taken, mate, John said, winking at Ben in the rear- view mirror. I stared at John. He wouldn't look at me. That couldn't go unpunished, I thought. I almost warned Ben, but then I decided it wasn't my worry.

I was suddenly aware that we were all waiting like lemons, all thinking about bloody Grace. I had the familiar feeling developing in my chest. I felt an extreme vibe about the day. A vibe that has never failed me. I was just getting out of the car when she appeared. She'd plaited her hair and twisted it round her head. I could see it looked adorable. She was wearing minuscule denim shorts, a red boob tube and platform sandals. They were all new things. Not wearing your black smock and Clark's lace-ups today then? I said. You have made an effort. Drive on, she trilled, plonking herself down next to a stupefied Ben. John brought up Grace's sinus- in-salt-water thing on the drive, but she didn't appear to know what he was talking about. Hoping for a master class, were you? I asked him. He answered with a blush.

Grace kept moving us on when we got to the beach. Ben was carrying all her stuff as well as his own, but he seemed cheerful. I decided to zone out. It was all too beautiful to feel ratty. The colours of the sea, the sky, and the dunes always seemed perfectly organised to fill my mind with a blissed-out sensation. Finally we settled, and I organised my things and watched the others. I hated all that faffing around with towels, losing your balance, exposing your bum to the seagulls, so I'd worn my costume under my sundress. Ben had his trunks on under his trousers. His legs were a bit pitiful; it seemed kind not to look too hard. John spent ages doing stuff inside his towel, which he struggled to hold with one hand while he took off his underwear. I laughed at him so much, he told me not to be childish. What on earth have you got under there that's so important, love? I said. No one cares, you know.

We lay down and arranged ourselves, and suddenly there was Grace. We all watched as she bent to pick up her towel. She had already been in the sea. Water coursed down her body. Her hair was dark and snaky, her small brown breasts were bare, each nipple puckered and nubbly. She must have timed this moment. I saw she was wearing the world's tiniest thong. Slowly she pulled the front of it down and exposed her pubic hair. The boys had become supernaturally still. I was beyond amazed. And not in a good way. Then she took her towel and began to wipe herself, patting the tufty mound of light brown curls. I had this feeling that we were all dazzled by her slow hand movements. She met my gaze without flinching. Anyone for a swim? she said, and snapping her thong back into place, she threw down the towel. I was about to ask where her bikini was, but it was too late; she had gone, running towards the sea. As she ran away, I saw her trailing it behind her. Both boys seemed to shake themselves, then leapt to their feet and raced after her. I picked up a magazine and tried to read. This was all so weird, but as I sat there I began to understand. Grace's transformation had so stunned me that my brain was slow in catching up. I shaded my eyes and watched the three of them in the surf. John tried to do a shallow dive and almost brained himself. I could see him weaving about, trying to look nonchalant while he rubbed his head. That gave me some pleasure. Grace was swimming like a mermaid out to a landing stage. It was as if she'd been taken over by some sexy, beautiful alien. It was still Grace's body – her hair, her voice – but more vivid, more potent, and even more tricky than Grace the silent, Grace the sarcastic, Grace the bookworm-girl.

I had to shade my eyes with my hand, but I could clearly see John attempting a suave over-arm out to the platform. I wasn't sure he'd make it. He was a rubbish swimmer. Ben stood in the shallows looking out to them for a while, then came back up the

78

beach and sat next to me. Got any sarnies? he asked. I gave him one of the pitta-pockets. Tomatoes were a bad idea. The soggy filling fell out into his lap. He seemed too depressed to care, even though he was going to have this horrible sinister stain across his crotch for the rest of the day.

Out on the platform John and Grace were sitting close together, their heads touching. It looked to me as if she was putting her bikini top back in place. Ben ate all my pitta pockets without asking, while we sat in silence and watched them.

John made it back to the beach eventually, his chest heaving. He almost collapsed onto his towel. I examined him as he lay there. His lips looked pale, as if he was about to faint. His body quivered. Are you okay? I asked him. Of course, he said, and laid his arm over his eyes. Pity, I said. For a minute I thought you might be going to have a coronary that would have been fun. Did Grace show you how to snort sea water? He blushed, but it didn't look cute at all. I couldn't believe I'd ever found it attractive. I could see Grace draped across the landing stage, sunbathing. She seemed a long way out. I ran through the sand to the sea and dived in. The water was like a wet version of paradise, clean and sharp, as it always is. She didn't hear me coming. I swam the last part of the way underwater. It felt as if the sea was pulsing along to the beat of my heart.

I could see her narrow foot dipping into the sea. I grasped it hard and yanked her off the platform. Then I held her under for a while. She struggled fiercely. I watched her sea- pale legs as they ran in slow-motion, feet like small hooks. I saw her arms move in decreasing circles, and the bands of hair radiating out from her skull like undulating eels. When I felt the time was right I let her up and bunked her onto the platform again. She sicked all over the place. I stood over her and watched as she sobbed and retched. When she was quiet, and breathing normally, I dived off and swam to shore again.

NEGLIGEE

In the office Grace kneels down to file papers into a metal cabinet. Holding a bulky file with both hands, she has one of those moments when everything seems to stop. She's had this feeling before, but each time is like the first time; it's as if she's bathed in a bright spotlight of silence. Her surroundings fall away; now all she can feel are the grey tiles she kneels on. She's next to the window, so she straightens up and looks across the flat roofs that shine with sheets of rainwater to the small hills on the horizon. In two weeks time I'll be a married woman, she whispers, concentrating intensely on each word. She waits, transfixed. Then the light fades, and Grace blinks and looks around. The engagement has lasted a whole year. To Grace it seems like a week.

After work, walking down the steps to where he waits, Grace sees herself walking down the steps. Here is Grace descending the stairs; her coat spreads behind her; her lover waits, she whispers. Look at Grace's seductive smile, see her wave. She looks up, tries not to scan the crowds, and sees him eyeing a woman secretly, sideways. Now she will not speak to him for hours. He won't know why. He'll call her his 'funny little thing', his 'silent mouse'. He'll tell her he loves her 'so much, anyway, even though...' Grace often thinks about these 'anyways' and 'even thoughs'; she understands what he means, but she doesn't tell him so.

It must be ten months since she tried to tell her father. On that night, she let herself in with her key. The house was in woolly darkness, her father sitting in his armchair in the far corner of the lounge. She opened the door and could see him, a darker shape, his hands in his lap. The curtains at the French windows were open and Grace could see his eyes. They were glinting with moonshine. The stars began to dance and multiply themselves in the huge mirror above the fireplace. Come in, Grace, he said, without lifting his head from where it rested on the back of the chair. Grace thought his head looked heavy, resting back on the chair like that; perhaps he was very tired, or depressed. She sat on the floor beside his chair, pressed her shaking palms together. While she tried to swallow the obstruction in her throat, her father had said how worthy her fiancé was, what a good husband he would make; he was someone she could trust herself to. It was God's will, he knew. She listened to his soft, deep voice in the dark, starry room. Now go to bed, Grace, he said; sweet dreams to you, dear.

Now it's the weekend. Grace is drying her hair in her room. She's washed it with a new shampoo; the smell of warm balsam surrounds her. It's reminding her of the pinewoods a long time ago. Grace sees herself in the woods, and imagines how the shafts of spring sunlight dropped down onto the forest floor, illuminating it in patches that seemed as if they might catch fire. 'Look at Grace as she runs through the burning woods, see the branch that crackles and falls, lighting her skirts as she races on'. Grace thinks about how everyone would look for her in the woods, try and bring her back. She can hear them calling for her. Her sister is flitting up, up in the beech-tree canopy, never coming down. Grace understands her family's calls, but she never answers.

Grace is ready to go out, but suddenly she feels weak and unwell, she doesn't want to go walking with her lover. She tells her mother so. She knows he will be thinking 'even though ... anyway, I still...' Soon the house is quiet again, and Grace puts down her brush, gets up from the dressing table and into bed, fully-clothed. In two weeks it will be my wedding night, she says to the empty room. The words float around like particles of dust. Grace reaches up and opens the window. She watches the words, still in the right sequence, as they are sucked out of the window. She wriggles her toes and begins to feel warm. She decides she will go shopping one day in the week for a nightgown and some perfume.

Grace arranges a day off. Things feel odd on the bus into town. All the ugliest people seem to be on the bus. The man in the seat in front has a rim of grease all around the neck of his jacket. Grace can smell the grease; it reminds her of something; she has to move places. She sits across from an old woman. Soon she hears the sounds of a violin, or it could be the sound of a crying baby. The old woman is holding a transistor radio to her ear. Her short legs swing to the music. They don't touch the floor. She has crimson, stiletto-heeled shoes on. She nods and smiles at Grace, beckoning. Grace thinks she must be very cruel to her children, perhaps even locking them up. Grace starts to feel sick and gets off the bus early.

Grace smuggles her bags of shopping up to her room. She lies awake until everyone, even father, is asleep, and then gets up in slow motion. The bags are in the bottom of her wardrobe. She doesn't switch her lamp on but lights a tiny candle in a cut-glass bowl. As Grace turns the bowl around in her hands, sparks of light are thrown up like streaks of water from a fountain. They splash the walls of the bedroom. Grace has never had her bedroom wallpaper changed. She wouldn't allow the felty rosebuds to be taken down; let her have her way, her father had said. She carefully places the bowl on her bedside table and opens the bag with the nightgown inside. The tissue paper says ssshhhh to Grace as she pulls it out. She lifts handfuls of the cold chiffon up to her face and breathes it in. Then she drapes it on the bed. This is the night gown Grace will wear on her wedding night; she will be so beautiful, she says. She lies down on it, gloating, and fingers the material. The colour is just right, like the sea, like a mermaid's cloak. No-one knows, but this gown is the very colour of Grace's eyes, she says, and this sea-green colour would be cool enough and wet enough to quench any blaze. She opens the box with the perfume in. The bottle sits in the palm of her hand, round and heavy. She holds the bottle up to the candlelight. The liquid glows. It's like the juice of an apricot or a pomegranate, warm and delicious. Grace thinks it could taste wonderful. As she holds the perfume bottle in her hand she sees the little diamond on her finger wink. She puts the things away.

It's the eve of the wedding. Grace is with her family in the garden. They are having a goodbye meal. The table and chairs are near the pine trees her father planted years ago. Now they are so tall they block out the evening sun. Grace's mother carries out the food, and Grace wonders if she even grasps that there is to be a wedding tomorrow, that Grace is leaving home for good. She puts down the food and goes back inside. Through the French windows Grace can see her little brother swaddled in blankets on the sofa. Her mother is feeding him titbits. To Grace the scene inside the room is so complete, so silent; it's like the view you might see in any stranger's house, if you walked past at dusk.

Now everyone is smiling and nodding, even Tamar. No one seems to feel the cold. Grace watches her father at the head of the table. He isn't smiling, but he nods at Grace from time to time, as if he's answering her questions. He is carving the meat. The smell wafts at Grace, reminding her of something. She gets up and walks away from the table, down the winding path her father laid, and stands amongst the ferns. Grace looks up to the mountain above the house. It is the shape of a shoulder lying below the sleeping sky. She thinks about the lake on the other side.

The asparagus fern has grown to reach Grace's ears. She kneels down and pushes her bare arms in amongst the soft stems. The ferns are waving, stroking Grace, soothing her. She thinks she would like to be small, about the size of a wren, so that she could make a nest lined with the frothy ferns. She hears her family call 'Grace, Grace,' but she doesn't answer. Soon they come and find her, take her back to the meat and the table.

Grace is walking down the aisle. Her sister is her bridesmaid. Earlier she sat on the bench against the pine trees in her wedding dress and waited for the family to be ready. Tamar had come out and sat with her, both of them in their long dresses. Tamar read a magazine. Neither had spoken; they'd just waited. Through the smell of pine Grace could sense her own perfume rising from inside the neck of her dress as her body warmed. She thought about its glowing colour and the facets of light in the darkened bedroom, about the layers of chiffon spread out on the bed. Grace feels she has turned her back on many things. This is the day Grace is getting married, she told the morning garden as she walked towards the beckoning asparagus fern. What she really meant was, Grace is getting away, never coming back. No one else came out to see Grace in the garden. They had stayed inside the house. To Grace her family all looked like more beautiful replicas of themselves. When she kissed them at breakfast, they felt unyielding, chilly.

Grace doesn't know she is making a small noise in her throat as she walks by her father's side down the aisle. Ssshhh, Grace, he says to her as they walk. She can't stop because she doesn't know about the noise. She is listening to the commentary in her head: see Grace gliding down the aisle, see how pale she is, how sea-green her eyes, how mute. There is a spotlight on Grace, a circle of silence she cannot break. Her throat is full of something. Everyone is waiting for Grace to say, she does. Her veil trembles, and then the silence is over. Everything flows now; there is no stopping it. Old ladies brush Grace's cool cheeks with moustaches. Someone feeds her chicken and fruit. Now she is being driven away. Look, there goes Grace, sweeping away on her honeymoon; see, she raises a hand to wave to the crowd. She moves close to the window of the car and follows the receding people with her eyes; she is looking for her father in amongst them. Grace cries in the car. Funny little mouse, her husband says and grips her knee too tight.

They stop in a little stone-built village. They are going to change out of these ridiculous clothes. The only place open is a tiny public toilet, reeking of urine, the floor shining with moisture.

Grace pulls off her pink going-away dress, and the toilet is alive with clouds of multicoloured confetti. Some sticks to Grace's eyelashes. For a moment she cannot find the door. They arrive back at the car together and drive on in silence, each in their jeans and shirts. None of this seems right, now Grace is out of her wedding clothes. She thinks of her nightgown, cool in its secret, sea-green folds, and the perfume she could drink if she wanted to, it looks so delicious. Here is Grace, careering through the darkening countryside, at the side of her lover. Her sea-green eyes have special powers. He turns slightly: are you happy, little mouse? he asks, not expecting an answer.

WHATEVER

Tamar's long fingers are steady, her nails like sugared almonds. He watches as she tears a polystyrene cup in shreds downward from the rim. She places the cup, splayed open like a sci-fi flower, in front of him. What d'you think? she says. He smiles and drinks the last of his coffee. Tamar looks at the way his throat works as he swallows. A strong, brown throat. Do mine, he says, and pushes the cup across. Tamar had decided when she woke not to try too hard today, just to flow, go with things – whatever. Anyway, it's the weekend; she has no plans. Here in the cafe she feels both passive and fully alive. The taste of the cappuccino, the rasping feel of spilt sugar under her resting elbows, the dry warmth of the polystyrene, his lovely throat, they all feel more than real. Perhaps hyper-real, she thinks, playing her favourite game – whatever.

He leans forward and talks. As she listens and smiles, Tamar watches him. He's asking about her family. She tells him she is an orphan and shakes her head; she has no siblings either. As soon as she's said it, she realises it's true. She doesn't pay much attention to what he says. There are things she needs to check, things that must be right. His hands, for example. He stops in mid-word as she takes hold of them and allows her to turn them palms up. She feels the texture of his skin. His hands are cool. She lifts them to her face and breathes deeply. Clean, indefinable smell. She rubs her cheek against his left palm and then licks it. No salt. A creamy hint of sandalwood soap. She would like to bite his thumb muscle. She places his hands back on the table. She knows he is surprised. Intrigued too. He smiles and asks, have I passed? She likes that he wears glasses. He tells her he can hardly see without them. He makes a joke of it. He manages to imply that this is an asset. She knows she will have to get him to take his glasses off. See how he looks. It could ruin everything. His eyes are bright blue, blondly long-lashed. He asks, should they have more coffee? Tamar decides no. They sit a little longer, reluctant to leave. Tamar is waiting; she doesn't mind what happens really. He asks her if she'd like to meet him later. I have to think, she says, and then after a short while she asks, for what? She feels only mildly curious. It all depends now on his answer. We could go to my place, he says, and stands up, reaching for his coat; have a drink. Tamar stands too. Or not, she thinks. Sometimes, she knows, the way she goes off with people has led to slight problems. Complications, so to speak. Do you like me enough? he asks, and waits with his soft black coat in his hands for her answer. Tamar thinks it will spoil her drifting time to tell him that. Instead she reaches up and kisses his chin. I've got things to do in town, she says. It's not a yes; it's not a no. He nods and suggests they walk together. Outside the cafe the light is failing, just the way Tamar likes it. Her coat floats out behind her. The trees that flank the path to town are dripping. There are heaps of slithery, dark- smelling leaves in the gutters, aureoles around the streetlights. Cars swish past, the sound heightening the silence Tamar feels settling around her. It's good he's not discomfited that she doesn't talk.

As they cross the road he holds her hand, their skin gliding, their fingers cold, almost too much to bear. Tamar is glad he didn't ask if he could do that. She would have had to say no. This way it's just happening, part of the day. He asks her what she will buy in town. Tamar hasn't thought. Shoes, perhaps, she says, purple, if I see them. He asks if they will have high heels. Tamar smiles sideways at him. Yes, she says, painfully so. Would you like that?

He stops and grabs both her hands. People walk around them. Here's what I want you to do, he says. Go and buy the shoes. Then, in an hour, meet me outside The Eagle Hotel. Yes? Tamar nods, and repeats ... in an hour... The Eagle. He drops her hands and walks away. She stands on her own in the darkening street, her legs weak, her throat aching. She feels adrift; anything could happen, anything at all. She's just going to let it. And that way nothing is ever your fault.

In a shop window in an arcade Tamar sees a pair of shoes she likes, but they are brown. Inside, she asks a black-clad assistant about the shoes. She doesn't expect to hear they have them in purple. It seems too unlikely. The assistant says she will go and look and glides away, her narrow skirt so long her feet are invisible. Tamar sits on a leather stool and waits, breathing in the smell of leather. She speculates calmly about the shoes; it doesn't matter. The assistant appears in front of her with a pair of shoes the colour of a rich, grapey bruise.

She kneels and holds them up in her open hands like an offering for Tamar to see. They look like something intimate, something that should be kept secret. Tamar thinks, if people see her trying the shoes on, they will know too much about her. Then she realises this is an alluring thought.

The assistant explains they are the same style as the pair in the window, but the heels are higher. Is this all right? Of course, Tamar says. They look at the shoes together for a few moments. Then the girl helps her to put them on. Now, if they don't fit, Tamar will know whether to meet him or not. The shoes fit perfectly. She wonders where he lives. A lot may depend on what his home is like. She's going to wait and see. The suede-and-leather feels warm, alive. They have straps across the ankles and tiny bronze buckles. The heels are high, perhaps four inches. The middle part of the shoe, the part that shows the arch of the foot, is cut away.

Tamar stands in front of the mirror and holds up her long skirt. The shoes make her legs look elegant, elongated. A mysterious woman's legs. The sort of woman to whom absolutely anything could happen. I'll take them, she says. The assistant wraps them in tissue paper and starts to put them in a box. Tamar stops her.

She wants to wear them immediately. She pays without registering how much they cost; it's not important anyway.

Tamar finds the shoes alter the way she walks. She feels aware of her hips moving, the play of the muscles in her thighs. It's addictive, this feeling. She feels like someone else, yet more herself than ever before. She has just enough time to buy a short skirt and finds one easily. It's purple velvet, with a swirling, imprinted pattern. She is wearing a white shirt. The skirt looks good with it. It's almost time to meet. As she approaches the hotel, she can see he is not there. It is exactly the time he said. Whatever, she thinks, and decides she will wait until the traffic lights have gone through three sequences, and then, if he hasn't come, she'll get a taxi home. It doesn't matter, she says aloud in the dark. The temperature is dropping, and Tamar's breath blossoms in a mist around her. It's starting to drizzle again. Tamar lifts the collar of her coat and holds it together beneath her chin. She is watching the traffic lights, determined to keep to her rule. As the red light blinks for the third time, she steps backwards and bumps into someone. He's facing the other way and pretends, as he turns, to have just noticed her. He's holding an umbrella. They stand close to each other, and he laughs. For you, he says, offering her the polystyrene flower she made earlier in the cafe. I was just leaving, Tamar says. I know, he says. Being under the umbrella is like standing in a room with the windows open. Tamar can hear the traffic only distantly. She recognises his perfume. She nearly tells him he's wearing her favourite, but decides against it. Still, the citrusy smell is welcome.

Tamar tells him she wants to have a drink somewhere neutral. Then perhaps, if they feel like it, they might go to his place later. He nods and suggests they have a drink in the hotel. Tamar follows him inside. The foyer is saturated with the smells of cigarette smoke, damp carpets and air- freshener. Tamar is intrigued; the place is so awful. He shakes his umbrella for a long time and then carefully folds it, bending over, absorbed. Whatever, Tamar thinks as she watches him. He is so busy with his umbrella,

89

he seems to have forgotten her. Feeling a snag of irritation, she walks away to the reception desk. There is no one there. She rings the electric bell, keeping her hand on the buzzer. The sound helps to smooth out her irritation. The place is dimly lit. He says, this used to be a good place. They stand waiting in the grubby foyer. Eventually a man comes down the stairs wiping his hands with a paper towel. He's wearing tracksuit bottoms and a T-shirt that has 'No Fear' printed on the front. As he walks toward them, he brings a wave of bacon. His lips are greasy. Tamar asks if they can get a drink. He says sure, sure, in an accent that sounds Eastern European. He gestures widely with his arms, flailing the stained paper towel. If you will be pleased to walk this way, he says, and leads them down an unlit corridor and in through a door quilted in satin. He flicks on the lights. Around the numerous mirrors there are strips of neon – green, blue and red. They flicker like the wings of flying beetles.

The hotel man reappears behind the grille of the bar. He struggles to unlock the padlock, and then with a flourish rolls up the barrier. He rests both hands on the counter and grins, waiting for their orders. Tamar decides she will have one drink and see how she feels. The bar, with its slippery banquettes and flimsy tables, interests her. She wants to have something very sweet and asks for Tia Maria. The barman takes a while to locate the bottle. The space he has to work in is inadequate. Eventually he finds it. The acoustics behind the bar amplify the noise of the bottle cap opening. Tamar hears the gravelly sound the sugar crystals make. He serves it to her in a half-pint beer glass and fills it to halfway. She tells him they'll share it.

The glow from the neon lights, refracted through the bevelled edges of the mirrors, sprays rainbows of colour onto the walls. The barman disappears. It's quiet. They sit and drink. His face has a blue neon tinge, and Tamar leans across and presses a red kiss on his cheek. He tells her she looks like one of the beautiful undead. I feel like it, she says. She drinks some of the Tia Maria quickly; her gulps sound unnaturally loud. She crosses her legs and for the first time he notices the shoes. In the electric light of the small room the velvety suede appears almost black; the bronze buckles wink. Tamar watches him looking at her feet. He has one hand, palm up, open on the sticky round table. Tamar places her spiky purple foot high up between his legs. Eyes closed, he moves forward, opens his legs wide and presses himself hard against the point. Now Tamar knows. Let's go to your place soon, she says. I need to lie down.

GRACE AND THE BASSET HOUND

On the motorway she watches a couple in the BMW ahead. As they overtake she sees the driver is a woman who appears to be shouting at the man in the passenger seat. Watch the road, Grace thinks; I'm not ready to die yet; but the woman is waving her arms about, turning sideways to face the man. She looks beside herself with rage. The passenger is immobile. Looking straight ahead. He's probably not even listening, thinks Grace – typical. She smiles to herself, acknowledging she's being unfair to John.

Beside her, John concentrates on his driving. It's a thing everyone takes for granted – John's wonderful driving. John accepts the unspoken truth of this. Grace drives with half her mind, like she does everything else. Not many people care to be driven by Grace, which suits her very well. John says Grace doesn't look ahead enough. Darling, he says kindly, sadly even (he hates to upset her, and anyway he knows she'll ignore him), you must learn to look ahead; read the road. Anticipation is everything. Grace knows all about looking ahead; she just doesn't care to do it. She glances at John. His perfect profile makes her want to touch him. Did you notice the people arguing in the car we just passed? she asks. Not now, my love, he says, and briefly squeezes her hand. I'm driving.

Grace turns the radio on. Van Morrison's singing one of their early favourite songs: 'Have I Told You Lately That I Love You?' John starts to sing along; '...ease my troubles, that's what you do...' His voice is light, he always sings in tune. He turns to look quickly at Grace, and they smile, sharing the song.

The traffic builds up as they approach the city. Buildings become more self-consciously grand and Georgian. John waits at a pedestrian crossing and smiles benign encouragement at the blank-faced woman hunched over a laden buggy. Grace knows he's taking care not to rev his engine and frighten her into a run. Without moving his head, he tells Grace he thinks she will like the hotel. Do we have to eat in? she asks. Not if you don't want to, he says, as he pulls smoothly away. I want things to be just right for you. He still smiles out through the windscreen, but Grace can see that he had planned to eat in the hotel. I don't mind really, she says, and puts her hand on his leg, strokes it, then leans across to rest her head on his shoulder. I do love you, she says, really I do, I do. You sound as if you're trying to convince yourself, John says. They get their arms tangled as he tries to change gear. Neither smiles. Grace notices that the air smells stale. She opens the electric window, and gets distracted by the open and close button. She starts to shut the window an inch at a time. Darling, John says, stop being naughty; I am trying to drive. Grace knows she is meant to say, okay, daddy, but she doesn't want to play anymore. She compromises and gives him a Lolita grimace, putting her tongue out. She can see he's satisfied.

Grace has been finding it increasingly difficult to concentrate. Things like the window mechanism have begun to distract her. They always have done of course. The difference now is that she allows herself to be distracted. Welcomes it. Slides into any little thing that takes her fancy. It's as if everything is new to her. What have I done with the past years? she wonders, as she relinquishes the window. I'm thirty, for God's sake; where's it all gone? She smiles at herself. Such melodrama. Such a waste of time. She looks at John. The breeze from outside lifts his dark fringe. Like a little kiss, the perfume he wears glances off her cheek. Grace thinks he looks tired. Washed-out. Washed-up. Nearly there, he says. Grace detests getting places. This was true even when they went on budget holidays. She always feels reluctant to leave the car, or train, or whatever else they have travelled in. She doesn't want things to begin. Travelling is undemanding; it has its own enclosed, self-fulfilling world. Then you get somewhere, and everything has to start. Even when she and John have been to beautiful places – places she's really wanted to see – she's felt the same. Now she answers John. Great, she says. He gives her a sideways glance, not taken in.

Grace thinks back to when they were first married. Her attitude was a problem to him then. He was the sort of person who never hung around to unpack. He'd get out his visitor's guide and book of maps and shepherd her around. Pointing out things of interest. Seeing the sights, immersing himself in the local landscape. Then later, when they could afford it, in some foreign city, taking in the local colour; all these things excited him. Grace first wanted to rest, have coffee, wait till evening; shower, perhaps make love on a strange bed. John would be puzzled. Disappointed. Like a puppy who wants to play and is rebuffed. They had eventually come to an understanding; John stayed with her, curbing his enthusiasms. Grace tried to make him go out on his own, but never succeeded. So then they were both miserable. As long as I'm with you, he said, that's all I care about. Now, as they turn into the hotel car park, Grace tries to envision when this had become a habit, not a preference. In the car park, a couple are getting into their big red car.

Grace can see a small bundle of fur jumping around inside. The woman lets a fluffy black dog out for a run. It sits still at her feet, waiting. Look, says Grace, what a little lamb. John has seen the dog, but as usual is not going to acknowledge it. Come on, darling, he says, we ought to get ourselves installed. Grace isn't listening. She feels again the familiar, irresistible desire to make friends with the dog and has walked toward the couple. She kneels down and strokes the dog. She can feel its heart beating quickly. She tries to imagine the dog's heart, what its texture would be. Could she hold it in the palm of her hand? The dog's fleecy coat is warm and black. There is a jewelled collar in amongst the curls. Just like a baby lamb, Grace says out loud, but to herself. The couple are indulgent. They tell Grace they worship their little dog. They understand her reaction. I want him, she tells them. They shake their heads and laugh. Grace is overwhelmed with love. The dog is docile; its shining eyes look mildly out at her from a soft ruff of fur. Its pink tongue looks to Grace like a tender slice of ham.

The woman picks up the dog, squeezing it gently to her.

Her ropes of creamy pearls click and glide behind the dog's floppy ears. His snuffling nose, a wet gleam, pushes up into the woman's neck. She gives a low, contented laugh. Grace pursues the dog almost into the woman's arms. Bye-bye, the couple say eventually, reluctant to take the dog away from Grace. As the car slides off, the woman holds her dog up and makes him wave his paw. John is waiting on the hotel steps, their bags by his side. He is studying a sign in the hotel window, his back turned toward her. Standing where the car had been, Grace feels bereft for a moment. Also she fears she has made herself look ridiculous again. She doesn't say anything about the dog to John as she joins him. He doesn't mention it either.

Grace loves their room – its white walls, the drapes at the open French windows, the white geraniums on the balcony, even the whimsical, wrought-iron furniture. She picks up a bunch of red grapes from a basket and rests them against her cheek. They're heavy and chilled. She puts two in her mouth. These must be the best grapes I've ever tasted, she says, as juice drenches her tongue. The carpets are springy, probably new, John says. He's walking about, opening drawers, investigating. The en-suite bathroom meets with his approval. He pours some mineral water and drinks it, swallowing silently. Grace watches him from where she lies on the huge bed, then covers her eyes with her arm. He moves to sit beside her. Grace, he says, I'm going out. She sits up, then understands, as she looks at him, that it's important not to comment on this startling change in behaviour. She lies back down. He strokes her hair, then bends and kisses her on the mouth. A long kiss. He's obviously found time to clean his teeth. His kiss smells antiseptic, fresh, as if it must do you good. After he has gone, Grace feels a rush of sympathy for him. She wants to cry, but can't. She lies there in the cool, pale room. It's true, she thinks, feeling a heavy dullness in her chest – hearts really can ache.

Grace feels a sudden need to be busy, domesticated. She gets up and begins to put all their clothes away. She hangs up John's shirts, burying her face in each one before she puts it in the wardrobe. She has chosen each one of these shirts herself. They all have a matching tie. What would John choose if she was gone? What colours would he wear? His purple cashmere sweater feels warm, as if he has just taken it off. It smells sharply of his cologne; she has always loved its cleanness. Now it reminds her of the first time they went abroad together. A month of hot, mute afternoons permeated with lavender. Even the wine and local cheese tasted of it – the wide, after-lunch silence intensified by a continual hum of bees and John's soft, sleeping breath. For a while Grace does not hear the distant sounds of traffic filtering in through the open hotel windows. She remembers John sprawled under a wiry stand of lemon trees, droplets of sweat like tiny opals on his brown skin. She'd stood and watched him sleeping. Just stood and loved him, not even wanting to touch. All around them hazy. Now, holding the sweater, she is shocked to recall how they felt about each other back then. Even though it isn't cold, Grace puts on the sweater and walks around the hotel room with her arms folded across her body. Her burst of energy has dissipated, and she lies down again and curls up, falling instantly asleep. Later, when she wakes, John is lying beside her sleeping. She looks at his face and tries to figure out what's changed. His mouth, she realises. His mouth is just as beautiful, but its mood has darkened. He's not so ready to smile these days. She slides carefully from the bed and takes off his sweater, then lies back down and opens her blouse, pulls her bra away so her breast is freed, then moves his head until he's resting on her. Don't worry about us, darling, she says. She rubs his downy ear lobe between

96

her thumb and finger. In his sleep he turns slightly and nestles his head closer. They lie together as the afternoon settles over them, turning the white walls to a feathery dove-grey. Grace can see their reflection in an oval mirror framed with a black filigree pattern. They look like lovers.

Grace becomes aware of the geranium's peppery smell. It is carried into the room each time a breeze blows the drapes open. John sneezes and wakes. I dreamt I was in my grandmother's kitchen, he says, sitting up. Grace waits for more. She wonders if he'll notice her breast. She wants to be kissed. She wants him to suck her nipples so hard she has to cry out, hold his head down. It's probably the geraniums, he explains, and gets off the bed to go to the bathroom. Why do you always lock the door? she calls. Habit, I suppose, he answers. Grace can see herself in the mirror: hair dishevelled, one lop-sided, empty breast hanging out at a peculiar angle. She looks like a dead body dropped from a great height. Don't worry, I'm not going to invade your privacy, she says briskly, straightening her clothes.

John unlocks the bathroom door and comes out carrying a huge bunch of white lilies. The shining dark leaves are startling against so many bright, open mouths. He walks over to Grace and hands them to her. The stamens are a bold ochre. As the flowers sway, they let fall drifts of pollen. Grace can hardly hold the thick stems in both hands, there are so many of them. Water drips down her skirt and onto her bare feet. John puts his arms around her and the flowers. For you, my love, he says, happy holiday. Grace smells the sap rising from the woody stems; the lilies seem to be breathing out a holy fragrance. I love them, she says. As she searches for a container, her arms tremble with the flowers' weight. She has to put them in three vases. Then she changes her blouse; the stamens have left dark orange pollen smears all over the front of it. She changes quickly, hoping John won't notice.

John makes them both tea and takes it out onto the balcony. They sit at the wrought iron table and look down to the hotel garden. It's the height of summer. The garden looks well tended but slightly parched, the colours a darker version of their June flowering. John points out to Grace that some of the bushes have berries already. A smell of wood- smoke drifts past. Grace feels hungry. I want to eat seafood, she says, idly. That can be arranged, John says, looking pleased. They finish their tea, and decide it's not too early to eat. Grace goes to shower. As she steps into the cubicle John's hand appears holding a slim blue bottle. A present, he says. Grace has the urge to pull him into the shower with her, and starts to tug his hand. He laughs. Darling, let's eat first, he says, withdrawing his arm.

The perfume from the blue bottle fills the steamy room. Grace feels it permeate her skin. She looks down at herself, almost expecting her skin to have taken on a blue tinge. She is glad to open the door to the bedroom. John goes to shower immediately, disappearing into the laden steam. He doesn't take long. Then they dress. This one, he asks, holding up a linen shirt, with these navy trousers? Grace nods. She puts on a flimsy, formless dress and doesn't look at John as she's doing so. Slipping into her sandals, she holds the door open for him. Will you be warm enough with that on? he asks. Grace is already halfway down the stairs. Don't fuss, she says, I'm starving. The dining room is furnished to match the bedroom. Wouldn't you have preferred a contrast? she asks John. Oh, I don't mind, he says; it sort of gives things a sense of continuity. She takes a sip of her white wine and smiles behind the glass. What? he says. Just thinking about your reply, Grace says. And? He's waiting for her to explain. Well, it doesn't surprise me, she says; but that's not necessarily a bad thing.

John's ordered lemon sole; Grace has scallops. These are fab, she says, and puts one in her mouth. The flesh is meltingly soft. It's like eating a virgin mermaid's buttock, she says, and takes two large gulps of wine, then has a short coughing fit. John watches her. Are you having fun? she asks him seriously, and holds his hand. Her fingers are dotted with parsley. John looks around at the other diners. Of course, he says. Grace is on her third glass of wine. I don't think you are, Jewels. Tell me you are. Say, Grace, you're an irresistible woman. I love you to distraction. I want to eat you on toast. Say it. John makes a snuffling noise. Let me eat my sole first, he murmurs, and chews quickly. Right I'm ready, he says, and takes a deep breath. Too late, my little gem, Grace answers, rising from the table; I need to pee.

As coffee is being served, John asks Grace if she's tired. Why? she asks. Just making conversation, he says. They decide to take their coffee out on the terrace. Grace orders a liqueur. Tell me, do you prefer eight o'clock to nine o'clock, she asks, as they get settled. And if yes, why? John wants to know if she means morning or evening. Evening, of course, she says. John considers for a while. Grace watches two squirrels in a beech tree across the lawn. She can't decide whether they're fighting or making love; could be both of course, she says aloud. Ah now, you said I had to decide on one or the other, John says, wagging his finger. Now you're changing the rules. Come on, is it a.m. or p.m.? Still watching the squirrels, Grace asks without expression, Darling, what are you talking about? John tries to suppress an exasperated noise. I'm sorry, says Grace, remembering. Well, either. It doesn't matter in the slightest.

They sit on for a while. It's beginning to feel cold in the shade. John suggests they go up to their room. Grace doesn't want to leave the bustle downstairs. Suddenly a picture of the bedroom forms before her. It reminds her of the other silent, white room. The room that seemed to wait, its walls quivering and crawling with leaf-shadows. Made over, eventually, into a study – something useful.

In the hotel hallway, Grace tells John she is going out for a walk. It's still so light and warm. The thought of spending time indoors right now is intolerable; she can't breathe. John goes into their room and comes back out with her jacket. He asks if he can come. They stand in the doorway. Grace explains that all she needs is a little time on her own. Behind John the bed seems to float and fill the room. He has already pulled back the covers.

On the pillow she can see a small, gift-wrapped box. I won't be long, she says, and turns away from him quickly.

Opposite the hotel, across the road, there is a park still open. Grace walks in through the gates. Browning rhododendrons straggle over the paths. The laurel leaves are filthy. It feels more like autumn to Grace. She can smell nettles and clogged drains. Everything will end, she thinks. And then it all begins again. It's a cycle. Everything is okay. In the breeze the trees drop heavy, black seedpods on her. She walks across the grass and sits down under a tall pine. She rests against its trunk. The bark is flaky, brick red. On the ground, millions of pine needles give off a herby, masculine smell that Grace likes. The lawn sweeps away from her, downwards. At the bottom there is a blind-looking lake with a single swan on it. Grace closes her eyes, trying not to think. The park feels abandoned. Then she looks up into the resinous heart of the fir and sees birds fluttering, settling, perhaps, for the night. The park is silent except for bird song.

She becomes aware of a movement near by. From around the side of the tree she can see a dog's head emerging. Oh, you big, floppy beast, she says, and holds out her arms. The dog is a Basset Hound. He's wheezing. When he sees Grace he stops and sniffs. His eyes are drooping. The bottom lids look as if someone invisible were pulling them downwards with pieces of thread. They look a little inflamed. There is some gooey stuff in the corners. Poor old fella, Grace says, come to mummy. Still the dog doesn't move. Grace makes coaxing sounds. She kneels up to face him. He starts to make a grumbling noise in his throat and lurches toward her. When they are face to face, he licks her nose and chin. His tongue feels like an uncooked veal escalope. It smells meaty. His saliva is salty on Grace's lips. Kneeling, she is taller than the dog, but he is longer, heavier. Grace thinks that, if she were to measure herself against his length, including his tail, they would be about the same size. As she looks into the dog's wet eyes, she feels that on some level they understand each other. What do you want? she asks. Tell me, I'm your friend. The dog lifts one squat front leg up and lumbers it onto Grace's shoulder. She is surprised. Do you want to get to know me? she asks. He lifts his other leg up and plants it on the other side. His head is above her, she has her face buried in the silky folds of his neck. The dog yelps and Grace can feel the sound move around in his chest. As his stomach lifts, his claws start to hurt her shoulders. Come on, boy, she says softly, off you get. She tries to pick his paws up off her shoulders, but they are so heavy it's impossible. Then he lets out a loud howl. As his stomach moves upward, Grace sees his penis appearing between his bandy back legs. She watches as it slips out of its hairy sheath and briefly rests, raw and shining, on the grass. Grace is gasping for breath, suffocating in wet fur. The chain around his neck clangs painfully against her teeth. Her arms are trembling with the effort of supporting the dog's weight above her. Finally, unable to hold herself up any longer, Grace falls backward and then twists sideways, trying to get out from under the dog.

The ground is pillowy with warm pine needles. She is blinded by clouds of resinous dust. Leaden, uncomprehending. Before she can get from her knees to her feet the Basset Hound has planted his front legs on her bowed back and forced her down. Panting, he noses his way up between her legs, scraping and clawing at the soft insides of her thighs. Grace is mute. If she inhales with any force she sucks in pine needles and sweetish, dry earth. She tries to hold her dress down. She tastes pine needles. The dog walks on her back with his front legs, trying to find a steady place, his back legs splayed and slipping. He stops with one front paw in her hair, the other on the ground by her ear. She can feel his penis drag across her buttocks. Once she feels him push against her panties, but he can't break through. Her brain blanks out, the dog growls, and suddenly she is conscious again. She feels him dribble, thrusting and thrusting. Grace lies still, making little moaning sounds, the muscles in her bottom clenched. When once she groans out loud the dog pushes harder.

101

Soon he slows to a twitch and collapses onto Grace's back. In a convulsive movement she gets out from under him and tries to stand. Her thighs are stinging. Semen as thick as frogspawn is quivering on her calves. She feels another patch in the small of her back. She gropes between her legs; her panties are intact; dry. Not in me, she says, shaking her head, no, not inside me. Her teeth are chattering; she's grinding grit. She puts her hand up to her ear. It bleeds; the earring has been pulled right through the lobe. She gropes around for her sandals and can only find one. She's crying like a child cries, mindless of how she looks or sounds, her mouth spiky with pine needles. I stink, she says quietly, and stops crying. She can hear again the evening birds in the branches of the firs. The dog lies still under the trees, his eyes half shut. She sees nothing as she walks back through the park. Then she is outside the hotel. It looms up out of the frothy garden like an ocean liner, throwing out cubes of yellow onto the bushes.

On the stairs going up to the room she falls, and sits where she falls for a while, resting her head on the wall. She feels as if every infinitesimal part of her body is trembling; the arches of her feet, the back of her neck, the roof of her mouth, her wrists. And inside, her ribs are vibrating; her arteries carry blood that judders as it moves away from her jumping heart. As she sits, gathering and un-gathering into her hands the torn hem of her dress, she starts to feel a different feeling grow inside her, as firm as the other is shaking. An absolute certainty is solidifying like a cube of water in the freezer. She straightens her back and continues climbing the stairs. Then opens the door of their room. It's like heaven inside: candlelight, champagne, everything white, white, white, and there's music, perfume. John is lying in bed, he has heard her approaching. He pulls the bedclothes back and shows her his narrow brown body, his white designer briefs. Grace can see, though her vision is wavering, that he has an erection. She rests a hand on each side of the doorframe. She can feel blood inching down her neck. It's no good darling, she says, it's all over.

PECKISH

Grace is just about to eat lunch. This could be one of the compensations of living alone, being able to eat when and what you want. Maybe it's good you don't have to ask someone what they fancy. Today she has made a big pan of lentil soup. She enjoyed crushing the garlic, chopping the onions. It's a ritual, soup making. It grounds her, makes her feel self-sufficient, in control even. The savoury smell floating around her white, uncluttered flat gives it a homely feel. As if things are going on. Lively things, normal stuff; some sort of family life. And you have to wait while the soup simmers, gets thick. You can't rush it. She thinks for that reason alone it must be good for lowering blood pressure. What d'you know, she says to the steamed-up mirror over the sink, wonder food. You don't even have to eat it, and it's doing you good.

Since she's been on her own, she's been doing things she never would have done when she was married. For instance, this talking to mirrors thing has developed. It's all right, though. Whatever gets you through the night. During those first weeks, all through a damply grey November, she'd busied herself hanging mirrors in every room. Several, in some rooms. That way you got treble, maybe quadruple the light, the possibilities. Each time she hung a new mirror up, it was like another bright window had opened onto a colourful scene, teeming with possibilities. These mirror-scenes were like old, illuminated initials, busy with movement. They added another dimension, more light. She couldn't seem to get enough light.

She is just taking two bread rolls out of the oven when the phone rings. It's her mother. Grace misses the edge of the kitchen table and drops the hot baking-sheet holding the crusty rolls onto the floor. Hi Mum, she says, watching the rolls bounce across the kitchen tiles. They scatter a disproportionate amount of jagged wholemeal crust and sesame seed everywhere. One spins under the table, the other veers away and does a somersault into the bowl of water she'd put down for the cat. What can I do for you today, mother? she says. She reaches across to turn the heat off under the soup pan. So will you feed your father for me? her mother asks. This is what her mother does. Gets on the phone and starts mid-sentence. No greeting, no how-are-you. Grace can hear her mother masticating. There never seems to be a time when her mother isn't simultaneously talking and eating. Especially on the phone. Grace tries to imagine what her mother is chewing. Cheese and onion sandwiches? A piece of home made coconut cake? She knows exactly how her mother will look. Blank-eyed, nibbling, nibbling. Her mouth puckering up, pale and secret as a baby's anus.

What are you eating, mum? she asks brightly. The chewing sound on the other end of the line stops for a moment. Her mother is swallowing. A corned beef pasty, she says. With Branston pickle. She giggles. It's an inappropriate sound. Now I'm drinking my cup of tea. Grace hears a series of gulping noises. Oh, for God's sake, she thinks, it's disgusting. Her own mouth is suddenly drenched with saliva. She forces herself to swallow. She takes a few deep breaths. She suddenly realises she could always sell up and move away. So, Mum, she says, where are you going, and why doesn't Dad cook something for himself? He's not paralysed, is he? I'm surprised to hear you take that tone with me, her mother says. She lets the sentence hang in the air. Then there's a deep breath before she carries on. Firstly, she's going on a two-day retreat with the Ladies Fellowship, and secondly, yes, she drones on, your father could fend for himself. Grace tries briefly to imagine her mother retreating from anything. Did you say fend? she asks. You make him sound like some tribal hunter-gatherer. This is Gwent, not the rain forest. Grace thinks about her dad. His trilby and Gannex mac. How, on the rare times he's left alone, he loves to eat sardines in tomato sauce straight from the tin with a fork; she called around one day and caught him. Don't tell your mother, he said, standing at the kitchen sink with the jagged open tin in his hand. Look, no serviettes, he said, smiling; d'you want some? They sat at the kitchen table, and he opened another tin for her.

She is aware that her mother is still talking. After all, Grace says, interrupting the flow, Dad only has to walk down to the chip shop. Her mother says again, more firmly, yes, he can fend for himself, but I don't want him to have to. Chip shop indeed. Grace knows she can't win; this is all too familiar. Still she carries on. But Mum, millions of people do it, you know. Do what? her mother asks. Go to a chip shop, eat chips, fish, the lot, Grace answers tiredly. Millions of people commit murder, says her mother. Doesn't mean we all have to follow suit. There's only you to ask, she says. No good asking your sister; she's never picked up a saucepan in her life. Except maybe as a weapon. Grace knows better than to mention her brother, who has temporarily fallen wholeheartedly into the ways of the world, giving her mother much cause to petition the Almighty.

Now, where were we? she says, and makes a tutting noise. Hang on a minute; there's someone at the door. It's probably your dad back from the shops. He forgot the list I gave him. Typical. I'll ring you back. Just as she's putting the phone down, she says, think about my request, please. Oh, and say nothing to your father. Then, at the last possible moment, she whispers, Grace, remember dear, I'm praying for your situation. I've put you on the altar. I'm waiting on the Lord for an answer to your ongoing relationship problems.

Grace's appetite has disappeared. She sits down on the single kitchen chair. Rests her chin in her hand. Perhaps she could hire her mother out by the hour. Guaranteed to suppress the heartiest appetite. Ladies and gentlemen, watch the incredible eating, talking woman. No need to go to the trouble of sticking your fingers down your throat. Just ten minutes exposure required. Special phone rates available on request. And an extra bonus – fast-track intercession on the client's behalf to the Almighty. No extra charge for direct access to celestial altar. No subject too small. That might be a nice little earner, she says to the mirror, now un-steamed. Her voice sounds unfamiliar. It's the voice she uses to talk to her mother. A plucky voice. She says *nice little earner* in a few different ways: first like a relentless TV ad voice-over, then like a female Fagin, then like a Sloaney, Kensington nanny. She does it just to assure herself the plucky voice is as easy to shed as any other.

She stares at the phone and wonders whether she could lift her mother up onto the altar. And even if she could manage it, would the Almighty be inclined to sort her mother out for her? She tries to imagine what would be a big enough incentive for Him. After all, her mother is an extremely devoted servant. He probably couldn't do without her. He definitely wouldn't be on Grace's side.

She stands up and goes over to the cooker. The soup has grown a thick layer of skin. It has become the colour of crumbling old bricks. Grace stirs it around, digging at the skin with a wooden spoon. It is surprisingly resistant. She tells the mirror above the cooker that she could repair the soles of her shoes with this soup skin. I could patent the idea, she says. She gets a fish slice and lifts the skin off in one piece. Some chunks of onion and carrot adhere to the underside. She lets it fall, heavy and wet, like a blood-soaked cloth, into the kitchen bin. She bends to retrieve the roll under the table. It has dried out completely; no warm, squeezable heart now. It crumbles away in her hand to fine breadcrumbs that look like sawdust. The other roll lolls in the cat's water, swollen to three times its original size. Grace thinks it looks like an elephant's dropping, though she's never seen one. Or a faulty, excised organ. She chucks everything – the bread-dust, the waterlogged roll and the semi-solid lentil mixture – into the bin. She opens all the windows and lets out the cooking

106

smells. Chill December air moves into the flat. She picks up her coat and keys and, switching the answer-phone on, without looking in a single mirror, goes out.

In town, Grace wanders. She has no plans. She goes into the market and makes her way to the pet shop. There was a time when she pined for a dog. It was a yearning she shared with her sister, strengthened by their mother's violent aversion to any animal they saw. She squats in front of the cages. Inside one is the sweetest Alsatian puppy. I can't take you home, she says, and strokes the puppy's twitching nose. Now she is alone and quite free to have a dog, she doesn't want one. It feels like too much responsibility. She'd be sure to let the poor thing down somehow. She acquired her cat by accident. You could hardly say she has a relationship with it. She can't stop thinking about her mother. The interminable eating. The way her mother is always on the lookout for something edible to tempt herself with. Years before, when Grace was small and they went out together, she'd ask her, d'you know what I fancy now? Guess what I fancy now. Grace could never guess. A bag of toffees, her mother would say, or a nice piece of ham and egg pie, or shamefully, a big bag of vinegary chips.

As Grace walks down a lane between two department stores, she remembers being sent into a chip shop while her mother waited around the corner. Put plenty of vinegar on, her mother always whispered. Then they'd stand out of the way of people, in a filthy alleyway like this one, while her mother ate the chips. Grace watched her mother eat, her own throat closing in as her mother's lips became shiny with fat, her thin and puckered mouth slick. Grace had to stand still and wait. Yummy, hmm? her mother would ask, and nudge her for an answer. It all comes back to her now, the gritty cold air of the alley, the smell of cooling chips. When they'd finished, her mother always gave her the cold, smelly papers. Get rid of these now, she'd say.

Grace sits in a cafe and puts her cold hands around a cup of tea. She is hunched over it. The steam plays around her face. She is remembering her mother eating a whole box of cheese triangles while she and her sister leant against her knees and watched, absorbing the delicious smell. She can see her mother unwrapping the thin silver paper carefully from each one, her fingers studded with small, pale blobs. And how she posted each creamy triangle through the narrow gap between her lips. As a little girl, she would go to the shops and buy her mother a big orange and a bar of mint- cream chocolate, or anything else her mother fancied. She remembers sitting on the carpet to watch her mother dissect the orange into juicy segments; then her mother would eat each piece, juice spurting down her chin. Grace can still feel the way her own mouth watered as she watched. Her mother never looked at her as she ate. She did not give a single segment of orange or anything else to Grace or her sister. Not for little girls, she'd say. It was one of the rare times she and her sister ever shared anything, and then it was nothing. It's four-thirty when Grace gets home. In town she's bought some bath oil, some thick white writing paper, a fresh trout and a chunky bunch of parsley. She feels she should be hungry, but the idea of the lentil soup still hangs heavily in her stomach. The trout may prove an antidote. She already has lemons and almonds. Later, when she's written some letters, she will surely feel hungry. Then she'll cook something light. Get back into the routine she's constructed. As she puts down her bag and coat, the telephone rings.

Grace knows it will be her mother, so she doesn't pick it up.

Instead she stands and listens to her mother talking on the answer-phone. At first it's difficult to understand what she's saying. There's just rustling and then a bang. Then her mother apologises for dropping the phone. She says she's juggling it with a bacon and egg sandwich. Then there's a pause as she takes a bite. Then slurping sounds. Grace turns away and takes her coat off. Her mother is saying, now, back to what we talked about earlier. Your dad's just gone back out. I didn't want to talk when he was around. Then there are more eating sounds. I just fancied a small sandwich, she says. Grace goes across to the window and gazes out at the darkened park, its lampposts with their blobs of wavering yellow light. She can just hear a dog howl in amongst the looming trees. The black flats are decorated with rectangles of light. Some lighted windows are uncurtained. Grace can see people, couples, families, moving around in their warm rooms. Her mother is saying it won't be difficult; you know he'll eat anything that's put for him, doesn't matter if it's unrecognisable or foreign. So you won't have to worry. As she says the word 'foreign', she seems to falter. Oh dear, she says, and starts to cough. Grace turns and stares at the machine. It is emitting choking, retching sounds. She is fascinated. Then she grabs the handset and says, Mum? Mum? There is no answer. Grace can hear thrashing sounds. She rushes out of the house and grabs her keys as she goes. Running down the stairs, she has to control a plume of laughter that wants to curl out of her chest. She realises her mouth is stretched into a broad grin. Stop, Grace, she says out loud as she unlocks her car door. It's not even remotely funny. It takes her less than five minutes to get to her parents' house.

She parks the car and fumbles for her door-key, leans heavily on the front door and, as it opens, stumbles forward into the long hallway. She listens, reluctant to move toward the lounge where the phone is. She sees her face in the hall mirror. Mum? she says into its shining surface. Only now, as she looks in the mirror, does her smile fade. She forces herself to walk and turn the corner into the lounge. There is a full-length mirror opposite her. Because of its angle, she can see her mother's legs reflected in the bottom corner; one of her slippers is off. Grace can see a hole in her stocking; her mother's big toe is standing up like a thumb saying, OK! Grace is terrified she will laugh again.

She moves around to where her mother is lying on the floor, her head propped up against the sofa. The handset emits a shrill tone. For a moment Grace thinks her mother is making the noise; then she realises no, and she picks up the handset and puts it back. She stands and looks down at her mother. She cannot move. She feels miles away. She feels not even her eyes will

109

move, but she takes in her mother's face: the patches of frilly fried egg littering her chin, her blue eyes staring. She's about to die, thinks Grace. She's dying, and I can't move. I don't feel anything. She toys briefly with the idea of leaving, getting in her car. She sees herself, out in the winter countryside. Later on this evening, she'll come back to the news. No one would expect her to know. She could delete the answer-phone message. Then she wills herself to fall on her knees and lean toward her mother's purpling face. As her knees hit the floor she registers that she's kneeled in the remains of the discarded bacon sandwich.

Her mother is making the faintest of sounds – the noise a motorbike makes on top of a mountain, carried down by the wind. Her hands are clenching and unclenching. Her knees tremble and jerk. Grace can see a snake of bacon rind peeping from the corner of her mother's mouth. All the while her mother's eyes stare into her own. She forces open her mother's mouth and pushes her finger and thumb down as far as they will go. She feels the back of her mother's throat filled with bread. Grace is following the string of bacon rind down. She has to push through the doughy mass. When she's gone down as far as she can go, she hooks around the rind and pulls. She feels her mother's teeth around her knuckles. Her mother's chest heaves. The bacon rind comes away in one piece, and Grace leans back to avoid the stream of bacon and eggs and coffee that comes with it. She shuffles further away and watches her mother as she starts to breathe and cry. She is holding her arms out to be held. Grace, Grace, she says. Grace sees her mother's tear-stained, sweating face raised toward her. She turns away. I'm sure you didn't fancy that, did you Mum? she says quietly.

WOOD

Briefly Tamar is alone and watches the waiter bring two steaming platters of food to the next table. She smells liver and onions, picks up a laminated menu and tries to concentrate on it. The liver-and-onion people have fallen silent. They seem to be mesmerised by their food. Without moving her head she can see that the woman eats by shooting her tongue out toward her fork and then reeling little teetering mounds of food in.

She remembers liver days when she was a child. The backs of her bare legs stuck to the plastic kitchen seat as she tried to cut offal into small, grey triangles. She remembers slipping them in through her lips. The liver crumbled like sour dust in her mouth. She smiles as she thinks about Grace retching like a fussy cat, tears flying from her eyes. Both of them getting sent to their rooms again. She remembers the precious one slurping up his soup and soft, floury rolls. Suddenly she wants to eat thin slices of cucumber and ripe tomatoes; maybe cold smoked fish and wobbly mayonnaise. The odour of next doors' food is the colour of gravy. She looks around for another table. There is something lumpy and not quite dry stuck on the menu. The words Go On, Indulge Yourself are partially obscured by what looks like a smear of French mustard. At least, that's what she decides it is. She puts the menu down. He is threading his way through the tables carrying two large glasses of white wine. I hope this won't be too dry for you, he says, and takes a sip of his. He follows her glance to the half-eaten plates next to them. Want to move? he says. They find an alcove by a deep leaded window. She can see primroses and pansies in the tubs outside. They look freezing, though the sun is shining. Her glass of wine is misty. It gives out a lemony glow.

111

There's nothing on the menu she would like to eat, but in the end she settles for a dish called calypso chicken. He says she obviously likes living on the edge. I'm not sure if that's true of me, she answers seriously, and pours herself some iced water. On the edge. She knows she has always been entirely at the centre of what matters. The ice cubes sound inappropriately musical as they splosh into her glass. Or could it be you just don't know yourself very well? he suggests, and finishes off his wine. She raises one eyebrow, but says nothing. When her glass is empty he goes to get two more without asking. She wonders if he's trying to get her drunk. This could end up being interesting after all.

The liver-and-onion couple walk past. The woman says something to the man, who nods. She thinks they are both looking at her unpleasantly, so she gazes at them until they turn away and disappear. When the meal is finished, he asks if she's had enough. More than, she says, and pushes her plate away. She sits up in her seat and places her forearms on the table. I think we should have coffee now, she says. Okay, he says, and leaves the table to order. Alone again, she closes her eyes. She can see herself standing on the bank of a vast river. She has an irresistible urge to sink up to her neck in the dark, fast-flowing water. She senses the sun on her face. Through the window she sees the flowers have stopped shaking. The light looks stronger. When the coffee arrives she briskly pours and asks if he would like milk. Are you always mother, he asks? Her hand is shaking as she holds the jug. I'm never mother, she says, and sends him a cool glance. Could it be sexual tension then? he asks. She looks at him. He's smiling at her. Definitely not, she says, and drinks her coffee, even though she doesn't want it.

They sit in his car. He has one of those wooden seat covers made of beads. Do you find that comfortable? she asks him. For a moment he doesn't realise what she's referring to. It's just that I've never understood them, she says. She thinks about the way her sister laughs at things like that. She asks if he bought them himself. He starts the engine. This car was my ex-wife's, he says. His face looks stretched as he turns in his seat to reverse; it was part of the deal.

They drive out of the car park, and she wonders where they are going. I thought we'd go to this beautiful place I know, he says. Secretly she looks at her watch. He glances at her. It won't take long, he says, and gives her the lightest touch on the thigh. What do you think? She feels the touch has pushed her back into her real life; suddenly she can actually see herself sitting in this car with him. She thinks about her empty house and calculates how long till there's the sound of a key in the door, a briefcase plonked on the floor. It seems impossible that it's all still there, in place, while she's here. She looks out of the window at the speeding hedges. I think that would be lovely, she says.

They travel for about half an hour. All the time they don't speak. She watches his hands on the steering wheel, and tries to imagine them touching her. His skin is dark compared to hers. She wonders what his brown hands would look like against her skin; she leans her head back and imagines them pushing her legs apart, his fingers inside her. They drive into a car park with stone posts. Beyond the posts she can see the beginnings of a beech-wood. How do you know this place? she asks. He says he used to bring his children here when they were little. That was all a long time ago, he says. There is one other car parked. Its windows are steamed up. They both look. She can see the back of a woman's head pushed against the glass. As the woman moves, she leaves a feathery shape in the steam. Through the wiped area of the window, she sees the woman's bare shoulder and looks down at her own lap. Someone's having a good time, he says. She turns to look at him. He is smiling, and frankly watching.

She waits for him to do something. He suggests they get out of the car. He goes and opens the boot. She stands on the brimming edge of the wood. She can see deep into its green heart. It looks like a place she might have read about in a book. Thousands of branches bend down and nod. Thin columns of sunshine flash on and off through the new, translucent beech leaves. Everything is quivering, although she cannot feel a breeze. The forest floor is smothered with bluebells. She can smell the wood's cool breath, ferny and sharp. Overlaying it all is the perfume of bluebells, so powerful is seems to be filling up her throat.

Shall we walk? he says, appearing at her side. He is carrying a small blanket. She decides not to say anything about it. They walk along a path. Wood anemones gleam in white clumps amongst the bluebells, accentuating their colour, making it purple. I don't know the names of many flowers, he says. Didn't you want to tell your children when you were here all that time ago? she says. Perhaps I knew then, he says; perhaps over the years I've forgotten. I can't imagine doing that, she says. Believe me, he says, it happens. He holds her hand. His feels warm and dry. He gently pulls her round to face him and kisses her cheek, then her closed eyelids, then her lips. He is still holding the bunched- up blanket. I don't know you at all, she says. What do you want? She doesn't feel like her usual have-all-the-answers self. It's like she's only half here, but at the same time fully into what's happening. She looks around her. Everything is shimmering blue and gold and green. Invisible birds are calling to each other. I just want to be your friend, he says, and kisses her again. She likes how unfamiliar his lips are. She turns away from him and looks down the bank. The flowers could be a frozen waterfall. There are ragged-winged cream butterflies feeding. He puts his arm around her shoulder and down inside her blouse. His hand covers her breast. She leans against him and feels her nipples harden.

She turns, pulls his face toward her and rubs his earlobes between her thumbs and fingers. She sucks his tongue.

They walk through the bluebells until they find a place where the soft, newly grown brambles have parted to make a little nest. She watches as he stamps the plants flat and spreads out the blanket. They lie down and gaze up into the mesh of sky and leaves. It's hard to take this in, isn't it? he says. He kneels, puts both hands up under her skirt and pulls her panties down. He raises them quickly to his face and breathes in, then puts them in his pocket. She lifts her bare knees and feels the breeze cooling her. He kisses her pubic hair and runs his tongue between her legs. Do you like this? he asks. She doesn't answer him. Instead she pushes his head down with both hands and opens her legs wider. She looks up into the trees with half-closed eyes. She thinks the sky could be water. Everything is mixed up. He tells her to turn around and kneel. She gasps as he forces his penis into her. The smell of the sappy, crushed plants is making her drunk. She pushes herself onto him, and he grips her shoulders. She tells him she wants him to come soon. Do it as hard as you like, she says, and lowers her head. She loves the noises he makes, his exuberance. He calls her darling as he comes.

CORDS

I'm lying in bed with my eyes closed. The memory of a dream is teasing me. I think perhaps if I'm perfectly still the dream could reappear. I want to get back there. The phone on the bedside table rings. I count to ten, then answer. I know immediately it's Tamar. Will I meet her today? she asks. We haven't seen each other for a long time. She's with another new bloke, I've heard. You could say things have cooled between us, me and Tamar. I mean, to the point where it's glacial. I suppose the cooling process started when she was born. She sounds really uptight, even for her. We agree to meet at the Arts Centre in town, at eleven o'clock. I'm just putting the phone down when she says, so you will come, won't you? Unnecessary to check, I think, and tell her so. Yeah, yeah, well, whatever, see you, she says.

I get up and go downstairs to make a cup of tea. I never eat in the morning; it makes me want to throw. So does coffee. Usually I need silence, but today I put the radio on and turn the volume up to max. My neighbour's deaf, so it's okay. I stand in the open back doorway, and the garden is beautiful. It's late summer, and the mint's been flowering for months; I don't pick it enough. I don't cook much anymore. I used to, years ago, but things have changed. I have a huge rosemary bush near the door. The tip of each spiky branch is a fizz of blue. In the sun it gives up a dark, savoury smell. The honeysuckle has bunches of berries so ripe and heavy they're slipping off the stalks. There's a slug as long as my middle finger desiccating on the sunny path. My empty shed is still new enough to smell. The warmth draws out of it a clean, uncomplicated odour of creosote.

In the shower I try to decide what to wear. I have my cup of black tea with me. I'm swaying about to some old song on the radio. The acoustics are great in my bathroom. Pity I can't say the same about the plumbing. I stand still when I realise the song is a track I used to love. It brings things back houses, rooms, people, meals. While I listen, I let the shower water fall into my half-empty cup, then, just as it brims over, I pour the cooling contents over my shoulders. I'm keen on the freedom of things like that, in the shower. Also, throwing the tepid tea behind me feels symbolic of something. I don't know what, but I feel better for it.

What I wear is important. Tamar always looks fantastic, though I'd never tell her so. She doesn't seem to try. I use some marine extracts shower gel. It's supposed to boost energy and enhance positivity levels. Bring that on, I think. I shave my legs as usual. Not that I'm wildly hairy. It's just that our mother made us swear a solemn oath when we were teenagers that we would shave our legs and armpits every day, *no matter what*. It was part of her religion. Almost as important as talking to God. The way she said 'no matter what' spooked me at the time. My fourteen-year-old heart was touched. Yes, mum, I vowed, I'll do it, *no matter what*. Tamar refused to promise. Whatever, she'd said; you two losers can vow what you want. I like my hair. And will the precious one have to shave when he's my age? If it weren't for the oath, I wouldn't have bothered today. I've decided to wear trousers.

I take thirty minutes over my make-up; it has to be right. My skin is good, thank God. And my eyelashes are long. I have a new bronze kohl eye pencil. I use it boldly. I'm wearing jeans and a low-necked black top with long sleeves that flare out and droop over my hands. I use a spicy perfume. I have on my long, leaf-shaped silver earrings. They look like two solidified tears hanging from my ears. I like it that they're heavy and tug my ear lobes when I walk. I paint my lips a bronze-red. Now I'm ready to meet Tamar.

The tables at the cafe are stupidly small. If you sit near, you might rub knees with someone, which isn't always nice. If you move away to get more space, you can't reach your drink. I usually end up with an ache in my lower back from leaning forward, but at least I don't get bruised knees. Or into a relationship with some weirdo. Its eleven-thirty and still Tamar is not here. I order a sparkling mineral water, but I don't drink it. Instead I try and interest myself in the contents of a display-case nearby. There is the most gorgeous sculpture of a seahorse. I love seahorses, so touchingly faithful. And the male gives birth; sometimes I almost believe in God. The cafe is nearly full. The smell of toasted teacakes calms me down. The sounds in the cafe are soothing. I wish I liked coffee. I wonder if I could manage to buy the seahorse. It's nearly pay day.

Tamar is in the doorway looking for me. As I wave and half-rise I drop my bag. Then she is at the table. She says, well, you look a bit fab. She doesn't kiss me. Tamar is looking thin. She wears a microscopic black mini-skirt and an expensive-looking black leather jacket. She seems ill. She sits and holds my hand briefly. Hers is quivering and icy cold. She orders cinnamon coffee and tries to roll a cigarette. I say, actually, no smoking. She looks up. So? she says. Who do you think will try and stop me? And smiles as she sheds tobacco into the sugar bowl. Shit, she says. I mean, literally, shit with sugar on, get it? I decide not to ask any questions. She manages to light her flimsy cigarette. She puts it to her lips and has a drag, burning it up to over half way. The woman on the next table pointedly waves her menu around, coughing. Tamar puts it out and rolls another, but doesn't light it. She used to hate the idea of smoking.

Okay, she says, thanks for turning up. I point out the seahorse sculpture. I love seahorses, she says, so faithful. Her coffee arrives. It's not strong enough, and she sends it back. The waiter she complains to acts as if she has just offered him a blowjob. He can't do enough for Tamar. He comes back smiling, a foaming cup on a tray. Is that better? he asks, and waits till she nods. Then he goes away. How do you do that? I ask. What? she says. She doesn't even know she does it. She picks at some dry skin on her top lip and makes a tiny raw spot. It bleeds. Shit, she says again. Weirdly, her lips look fuller than they used to. The patch of deeper red suits them. My eyes are drawn there repeatedly. This could take a long time, I think, so I order a pot of tea.

I don't send it back though; I have a jug of hot water to make it weaker, how I like it. Since when no sugar? Tamar asks. She's always talked like that to me, in shorthand. A couple of years at least, I say. That shuts her up. She rubs her eyes with her hand; the newly fragile fingers droop limply, the bones from wrist to knuckle like a fan. Her nails are painted with almost black polish. She's crying and trying to hide the fact. I'm shocked. Tamar doesn't cry. Order me a teacake, she says, sniffing. I order two. We wait for them to arrive. She holds out her hand to me. I go to clasp it. Tissue, she says; I need one. A different waiter brings our order. This one also hangs about the table; he can sense something's going to happen, perhaps a scene. I don't blame him. I've done his job, and it can be terminally boring. A blazing row can brighten the whole day. Our teacakes smell like heaven – spicy, buttery, wholesome. Almost I wish I could take all that comfort and spread it on Tamar. Or better still, on myself. We don't eat.

It's enough to have the warm teacakes here on the table.

Tamar looks as if she might speak soon. I feel as if some large mammal is resting on my chest. It's a warm feeling, but restricting. Drink your coffee, I tell her. She holds the large cup in two hands and drinks. Her throat works convulsively with each swallow, as if it were sore. She has a tiny silver nose-stud in the shape of a fish, and there's a ring on her wedding finger. They're both new to me. The ring's chunky silver with a square green stone. It hangs loosely, and the stone slips round to rest in her palm. All these unfamiliar accessories make her even more of a stranger to me. She puts her cup down but doesn't raise her head. Her long, straight hair shines. It quivers with the shaking of her body. The sight of it fills me with a sense of our long-ago, not-really-shared life. It reminds me how things have changed for both of us. I feel a brisk wave of nostalgia washing me clean. The unpleasantly warm, tight feeling in my chest dissolves. Tamar holding back is a new thing. Come on, I say. Tell me what's going on. She doesn't look up. I know you're going to say I'm stupid, she says, and you won't want to listen to me. Since when has that stopped you saying anything? I ask her; but I shake her arm, to make it less harsh, which is new for me. True, she says, lifting her eyes to stare at me. God, I say, so it's brown eyes now? Got bored with blue? What are you, a replicant? Contacts, she says. They give me a new outlook on life, and keeps on staring. Oh no, I say, don't tell me it's the dream. Surely that's not what this is all about?

She pushes her hair behind her ears. It makes her look young and recognisable to me again. No, she says; it's changed now. Well, it's the same, but different. It's our old, synchronised dream, but now it means something else that makes me scared. I've been having it every night. But not last night, or the night before that. I stayed up, smoked some stuff, drank myself stupid. Her eyes liquefy. But isn't there anyone with you? I ask. She looks at me squarely. I'm alone, she says, and I'm afraid to go to sleep. Then she hesitates. Go on, I say, tell me everything.

She says the dream starts as usual. We're in our house, the enormous house that's always the same. You remember? she asks, and I nod. We are there expecting someone. And sure enough, there's the table, like something from a monastery, long enough to seat thirty people. But we're not serving food. We have a daughter, very young. She's just the same as before, only now she's about fourteen. Sweet, pretty, blonde. We love her so much. We are sitting at the table waiting. She is coming home soon. All we can do is sit. This is the difference: tonight she is going to give birth. We are going to help. Tamar tells me these things as if she's pleading with me. I realise I'm holding her hands across the table, as if she is in danger of being swept away.

Okay, she says, wiping her eyes, then someone drops our daughter off at the door. I don't know who. We hear the sound of a powerful engine as it revs and fades away. Then she is in the room, standing at the table. She has twigs, beetles, spiders in her hair. Her feet are bare and bleeding. Mother, she says, and holds her arms out to us. She has been crying. Her little face is streaked and swollen. She is heavily pregnant. We speak gently to her; the room is filled with an unbearable sadness. We have warm, scented water in a bowl, and we wash her damaged feet. Have you walked far, dear? we ask, but she is mute. Lie down, we say, lie down. She is in pain. We lift her onto a bed. As she sinks into the blankets, we see it is a cradle. She gazes up at us, and she looks like you, and she looks like me. Ssshhh, we say, everything will be all right. We know the baby will be born tonight. We watch her as she falls asleep. Then we lift a heavy wooden cover and place it over the cradle. Now it is a coffin.

We light all the candles we can find and climb up to sit on the coffin lid. We listen, we strain to hear any sound coming from inside. We read from big, dusty books. We tear out and eat some of the illustrated pages to gives us strength. All but one candle goes out, and then we hear her call from below us. We lift the lid and look inside. There is blood everywhere. Our daughter looks sullen and ugly. Her eyes are shifty. She reaches down and pulls something out from between her legs. We soothe her and hold the dripping child. You say, there, everything will be fine now; things will work out. But the baby is strange. We see it is small, very small.

About the size of an adult's hand. We realise things are not right. But we have to reassure our girl. The little creature has no eyes. It looks like a grub. Despite these things, we love it anyway. The umbilical cord is still attached; it has all the baby's organs suspended from its length: fat kidneys, dark liver, lungs like branches of pink coral. They all hang off the dark-blue cord like some living necklace. The cord is as heavy as a ship's rope. It runs from our daughter's body, between her legs, to the baby's mouth, and from the baby's mouth to her mouth again. The creature has no lips, but we have to cut the cord. Even though the creature will surely die, we've got to cut the cord. But we know it's very strong. We know it is indestructible.

121

I become aware again of the sound the cappuccino machine is making, and the tinkling of spoons. Briefly I don't recognise them. My sister and I are holding hands tightly; it's hard to say whether we are trying to extricate ourselves or hold on. We are both crying silently. I look around; several people are staring at us. The first waiter who served Tamar is walking toward our table, his eyes fixed almost hungrily on her face. I turn to look back at her. She obviously has no interest in our surroundings. She will not let me go. In the dream you tell me we have to cut the cord, she says. She squeezes me even harder, the now brown of her eyes glittering with tears. But you see, she says, shaking my clasped hands, this cord, we can we never break it, can we?

ACKNOWLEDGEMENTS

Some of these works first appeared in *New Welsh Review*, *MsLexia* and *Planet* magazines. Acknowledgements are also due the following anthologies: *Mr Roopratna's Chocolate* (Seren) *Ghosts of the Old Year* (Parthian) *My Cheating Heart* (Honno) and *Eagle in the Maze* (Cinnamon). 'Negligee' has been broadcast on BBC Radio 4 and the World Service. 'Radio Baby', 'The Point' and 'Stones' have all been winners in Rhys Davies competitions. 'Kissing Nina' was shortlisted for the Asham Award.

I would like to thank the Arts Council of Wales for the writer's bursary I received to complete this book.

An earlier version of this book, together with critical commentary, was successfully submitted for the Ph.D. at Cardiff University. I want to thank my supervisor, Dr Roger Ellis.

Thanks to Jane Blank, Karen Buckley, Anne Cluysenaar, Bryn Daniel, Colin Evans, Danny Gorman, David Greenslade, Hilary Llewellyn-Williams, Liz Porter, Ruth Smith, Claire Syder and Jim Tucker.

Special thanks to Victoria.

This book is dedicated to Norman Schwenk.

SERIES EDITOR: DAI SMITH

WWW.THELIBRARYOFWALES.COM

Parthian Fiction

Hummingbird
Tristan Hughes
ISBN 978-1-91-090190-8
£8.99 ● Paperback

Winner of Edward Standford Award

Ironopolis
Glen James Brown
ISBN 978-1-91-268109-9
£8.99 ● Paperback

'A triumph'
– The Guardian

Pigeon
Alys Conran
ISBN 978-1-91-090123-6
£8.99 ● Paperback

Winner of Wales Book of the Year

Winner of Rhys Davies Award

The Long Dry
(Granta edition)
Cynan Jones
ISBN 978-1-78-378040-2
£8.99 ● Paperback

'A convincing glimpse of life,
in all its beauty and its sadness.'
– Big Issue

PARTHIAN